THE
NEVER
TALES

PRAISE FOR THE NEVER TALES: VOLUME ONE

"This is a retelling anthology with a lot of range. The talented authors all bring their own versions of this story to life. Between the beautiful prose and fun poetry, there was never a dull moment."

- Nathaniel Luscombe,
Author of *The Ones with Gilded Bones*

"This collection of retold stories and poems is not the one you would read to your children in the nursery. These are stories about the monsters lurking outside the window and within the shadows, tales about love, betrayal, revenge, determination, and hope. *The Never Tales* is chilling, enthralling, and sometimes whimsical...speaking to the child in us all."

- Everly Haywood,
Author of *Peaceweaver*

THE NEVER TALES

VOLUME ONE

Hannah Carter • Anne J. Hill • Beka Gremikova

Lara E. Madden • Emily Barnett • Maseeha Seedat

Julia Skinner • Tasha Kazanjian • Annie Kay

Cassandra Hamm • AJ Skelly • Rachel Lawrence

Brittany Eden • Charissa Sylvia • Jade La Grange

Savanna Roberts • Rebekah Crilly • Kayla E. Green

THE NEVER TALES: VOLUME ONE

Paperback ISBN: 978-1-956499-08-7
Edition one published in August 2022
Published by Twenty Hills Publishing

Cover Art by Real Life Design Covers
Interior formatting by Dragonpen Designs
Publisher logo by Nathaniel Luscombe

Edited by Hannan Carter and Anne J. Hill with help from
Maseeha Seedat, Rachel Lawrence, and Brittany Eden
Book created by Anne J. Hill, head of Twenty Hills Publishing,
with the help of Hannah Carter

CONTENT WARNING:

Fantasy violence
Murder
References to sexual violence
Physical, emotional, and verbal abuse
Suicidal ideation
Gore
Violence against children
Death
Cannibalism
Swearing/Vulgar language

Hannah Carter:

To my grandmother, Pam—thanks for not letting Faith dissuade me from believing in Peter Pan. You were a valiant defender of my daydreams. Because of you, I never left Neverland.

Anne J. Hill:

To Kat, my cousin, for her birthday. I love that you embrace your inner child and know how to have fun. Love ya!

TABLE OF CONTENTS

INTRODUCTION

ACKNOWLEDGMENTS

ABOUT THE AUTHORS

INTRODUCTION

WHAT APPEALS TO us about Peter Pan?

From a young age, I, Hannah, always found Pan fascinating. Perhaps it started with the Disney movie, or maybe it started because my parents would play *Neverland Medley* by Kenny Loggins as a lullaby every night. But, whatever the reason, Peter soon became my closest imaginary friend.

I spent many nights star-gazing, hoping that if I could only find the second star, Peter Pan would whisk me away to Neverland. And the older I got, the more I wished that he really would come to me because never growing up became more and more enchanting.

Really, I think those are some of the reasons that Peter Pan has found such universal appeal.

Often, Peter is portrayed as a friend to the lonely. He represents a found family, a place where outcasts are accepted. Where those that might not have friends are welcomed with open arms to the tribe of Lost Boys. He represents the beauty of childhood fantasies—mermaids, pirates, fairies—a place we can explore endlessly. And we never have to face the ticking clock—unless it's inside a croc!—and grow into those hideous creatures called *adults*.

But Neverland also carries a darker side—even J.M. Barrie knew that. I do not believe he meant Peter to become the hero he is today. Indeed, in the original play and book, there are hints at Peter's darker nature scattered throughout. Barrie somehow managed to mix the appeal—and, in some ways, benefit—of being a child forever without glossing over the more dangerous aspects. Children can be selfish. Children do not think about consequences. Immaturity and infantilism can be unwanted side effects of "Peter Pan Syndrome," and a preoccupation with staying young has permeated our culture in many negative ways.

What, then, are we to do? Forsake childhood altogether so we don't fall into the dark depths and never leave, never grow, never mature?

Heaven forbid.

Perhaps this book, and Volume Two, which will come out later, are good starting places for what the ultimate goal can be for those of us who feel like starry-eyed travelers, those of us who still believe in faith, trust, and pixie dust. Just like the original *Peter Pan* itself—and even Barrie's own life—*The Never Tales* appreciates that precious sweet childhood whimsy . . . and also the fact that there are man-eating crocs in these waters. Perhaps we can give you memories to cherish—while teaching you how to fight off the demons in the dark so you don't have to be afraid of your own shadow.

So turn on your nightlights, tuck yourself in—because Peter always comes for his Lost Boys.

—Hannah Carter and Anne J. Hill

LOST NAMES

Hannah Carter

ONCE UPON A time, someone asked the question: what's in a name?

And I know the answer.

Everything.

And nothing.

For you see, in the past, I have gone by many names. Each name was nothing more than a mask I wore to suit whatever purpose I had.

To inspire fear, I used the name Baba Yaga, among others. Fear has always been such a good motivator for humans. At every bump in the night, they were willing to give me whatever I wanted to appease me.

Sometimes, though, I needed to use finesse. Outwit them. Charm them, even. Because when humans feel they have risen above such a primitive, base emotion as fear—well, someone needs to remind them that there is *much* more to fear than just fear itself. Someone more intelligent than them. Someone more powerful than them.

And so, I used the name of the Pied Piper to get what I wanted. I could trick them and disappear into the annals of their history, a name with no face. A threat that became a legend.

And still, I am the winner.

But the citizens of London grew complacent. They believed that all the old threats and fears their ancestors harbored had disappeared with the turn of the twentieth century.

It was my job to remind them that they were arrogant fools.

But I had one setback since my last name had been stolen from me: the lack of a human host. In my true form, I was nothing more than the dark shadow of a wolf, a herald of winter, of cold and hunger, but unable to impact the world as I could as Baba Yaga or the Pied Piper. Without a name, without a body, mothers and fathers could soothe their children after nightmares, tell them that I could not hurt them.

A snowflake escaped from my mouth and froze a weed that dared to poke its green head out of the dark London streets. Yes, let the children believe the sweet lies that I was nothing more than the monster under the bed—it made it much easier to possess them and use them as my human hosts.

I slipped through the winding London streets in darkness. All sorts of emotions drifted on the night air to guide me. Oh, so many tantalizing ones. Wrath. Betrayal. Sorrow. Fear. They would certainly sustain me, but I grew tired of their dry taste on my tongue.

A sweeter smell ensorcelled me, much more poignant and flavorful than any of those. Yes, I could bend all the other emotions to my will, but it was too simple.

I smelled a prey much more satisfying.

Loneliness.

It drifted most potently from a two-story house.

I slithered up the ivy-covered stone wall to the open window. A young boy, barely out of his first decade, sat cross-legged on the floor. Tears stained his cheeks, and he sniffed as he trailed his hand below his nose. He clutched a pirate figurine with a missing hand.

The house was silent, save for sniffles and the loud *tick-tock* of a clock downstairs.

And then my voice.

"Home alone, child?" My voice was soft, soothing—no need to inspire fear or coerce this one. Lonely ones responded best to a listening ear.

The boy in the green shirt nodded. His eyes widened as he caught a glimpse of me on the floor. "Mmhmm." He shivered as a trail of frost formed behind me.

"Where are your parents?"

The boy stroked the wooden face of the sword-wielding swashbuckler. "I don't know. Out. Always are."

I murmured in sympathy. "Poor thing. If only you had some friends that might keep you company." I tasted vague impressions of his memories through his emotions. "But your schoolmates . . ."

The boy's face crumpled, though he didn't dissolve into hysterics. Neither did he have any words, but unbridled loneliness rolled off him in droves. So saccharine and potent—like chocolate that melted in your mouth.

"No schoolmates, either?" Emotions are so delicious, so mouth-watering, so *telling.*

"I'm better by myself," he finally said.

Delectable resignation. So young, and yet, so broken. Life had stolen this boy's light before he could even reach puberty.

I loved it.

"Are you?" The candlelight flickered as I spoke, and I grew and shrank in its glow. "Tell me, boy. If you could have anything, what would you want?"

The boy tucked his knees up to his chin. Hope flickered across his face before he squashed it—such a good little trinket. Already, half of my battle was over. Someone who had learned that hope only leads to disappointment was ready to lap up all my machinations.

"Nothing," he whispered.

"Really? Nothing?" I circled him. His eyes followed my movements, but he didn't shudder. The lonely subconscious is open to any hint of fellowship, no matter how odd. "Not even a friend?"

"No." The boy shook his head. "No friends." But he tilted his head and stared down at the painted face of his plaything. "Maybe more toys. More pirates. Maybe a crocodile for them to fight!"

Excitement crossed his face.

"Toys are safe," I agreed. I could sound congenial when I desired. "They can't hurt you. They can't leave."

The boy considered my words. Digested them. Inclined his auburn head. "Yes."

"But . . ." My promise lingered in front of him. "What if I told you I could find you friends that would never leave?"

His face darkened, and a wave of anger rolled off him, so potent—a three-course meal for me. I greedily slurped it up.

"Then you'd be a liar. Because anybody who says they'll never leave is lying." The poor boy gripped the trinket in his hand so tightly that I thought the head might pop off. "I know. Even Nanny Trudy grew up and got married and left me."

I circled him—a vulture surveying its prey—careful not to touch the pirate. I was unsure if the sword was made from iron or silver, and the latter made me wary. "But I can make you a deal. I can give you friends that will never leave you. Never grow up. Never abandon you. What do you say?"

The boy shook his head.

Ah, how pure it is to cling to innocent heartbreak instead of the promise of hope.

I heard the front door open.

"I'll come back," I assured him. "Don't worry. *I* will never abandon you."

And I kept my promise. Whatever names one might call me, one cannot deny that I was an honest creature when it suited my needs.

After all, did I or did I not get rid of those rats, just like the beggars of Hamelin asked me to?

Night after night, promise after promise, I filled that poor boy's lonely nights. I delivered toys and goodies, spun stories to elicit more emotions.

"You know," I began on one such night. "I know a place where no one *ever* grows up. We could go there."

"We could?" The boy shivered.

"We could. And we could bring as many people as you want." I rustled his figurines that were set up in line. "And have adventures. With mermaids, fairies, pirates—*friends*."

The boy swallowed. A tear slipped down his cheek until it froze from my breath.

Then he uttered the words I needed to hear: "All right. I want you to take me there—and give me friends that will *never* leave."

I licked my fangs as if I could already taste the first meal I'd have once I merged my shadow with this boy's, took over his husk, and inhabited his mind through that dark connection.

"No matter the cost?" I whispered in the darkness.

"No matter the cost."

The next evening, I slunk through the alley, dressed in the boy's skin. His consciousness slumbered in the back of my mind. Perhaps he would wake and fight me. Sometimes hosts did, but he was so small. So innocent.

I smiled the boy's smile, though I wondered if anyone could see the wolfish shadows lurking on his face—the twisted satisfaction hidden behind his lips.

I turned onto a main street, the sun already painting the sky varying hues of pink, orange, and yellow above me. No one paid attention to a street urchin. Perhaps they thought I was just a friend as I goaded young children to follow me. Perhaps onlookers thought I was just an older brother as I loomed over the prams of babies when nannies weren't looking, out for one last walk before they were whisked off to the nursery.

I snatched them off instead.

That first night, I stole three new friends.

But what would the paper think? They would call me a child snatcher, and then everyone would be on guard. People would hunt for the culprit with the ferocity that they hunted Jack the Ripper, and if they traced it back to me, my new name and face would be ruined.

So I whispered stories into the ears of the distraught nannies.

I planted the seeds of a magical world inhabited by pixies and fairies and these strange children. I hummed lullabies and songs, infiltrated nurseries and dreams. The children were not *gone* or *taken*. They were merely *lost*.

More and more children wished to come to me. More and more children left their windows open and murmured my new name in bedtime prayers. Soon, all it took was one visit, and small ones would flock to me, even easier than when I'd twisted the tune of that minstrel and lured the babes of Hamelin out of the city.

Deep in the forest, we played.

By the shores of a lake, we played.

Hidden from all others, running wild in the trees, away from the world, we played.

Pirates and mermaids, fairies and crocodiles. Anything my host could dream up, I gave him using his imagination and a world of my own crafting. The joy of such innocents kept me entertained, and the little mishaps kept me sustained.

Like the one instance when one of the boys lost a hand.

I gobbled it down that night, my first taste of flesh in years.

Perhaps I got greedy after that.

But children's flesh—so supple, sweet, not yet tainted by adulthood—was my true sustenance, flavored by the emotions I yearned to feast upon.

My host was easy enough to manipulate.

Through my influence, he stayed younger than he ought. But I could only be a parasite to one person at a time, which meant that the lost ones I'd stolen did not have the same blessing.

They changed.

They morphed.

They *grew up*.

And to grow up meant to desert childhood, something my host could not allow.

Funny, no matter how many promises I fulfilled, he was never truly content. He merely became more desperate to keep it, to fill the loneliness inside him, as permanent a feature on him as the green shirt he never outgrew. These friends became the dirty rags he shoved into the hole in his heart to stop its bleeding, but the thought of "how long until they inevitably fall out" always consumed him.

And I could use this to torment him even more.

"They're going to abandon you," I hissed one night as he tossed and turned in bed. "They will go away, just like everyone else did. Let me get you new ones. Leave these older ones to me."

For I had fed them a steady diet of things that I loved to taste, let their emotions run unchecked, like how one might soak a chicken in a desired sauce. My mouth drooled as I circled the boy's consciousness. "*I* will never leave you."

He allowed me control, as he often did.

And so we began to thin out the crowds. The eldest boys fell to me to do what I pleased with, and I stole my host's memories so that he would not remember their existence. No, to him, everything must be as it once was. There could be no growing up, no abandoning, no changing.

And for the others, the families left behind? Deceived by the stories I spread, they believed their missing children were actually in a better place, a place they longed to go, as well.

Such blissful ignorance all around.

So when did it all go wrong?

When that blasted girl entered the picture.

She was one of my most ardent admirers. The boy often perched outside her window and listened to her weave magnificent adventures. I lurked in the back of his consciousness, tasting her joy as she spoke my name, the idolization that whet my appetite. The boy, I could tell, had found another dirty rag to stuff his heart-hole with. He begged for me to whisk her away. I acquiesced.

After all, her sweet nature would make a rather delicious dessert in a short time.

So I slipped in, wearing the boy's skin.

I lingered over her bed until her eyes flew open. She gasped, her hands flying out, perhaps to throttle me, but she held back when she noticed who I was.

"You," she whispered.

I nodded. "Me."

"I knew you were real." She sat up, and I moved back so we did not collide. She bathed me with exuberance and joy, her childish excitement at my very presence a salve for my soul. I resisted the urge to inhale deeply. During my time as Baba Yaga, I had learned that, for some reason, humans do not like to be sniffed like they are going to be dinner.

"Of course I'm real." I perched on the end of her bed, legs crossed in a carefree manner. After all, I had never been thwarted when I went by this name. What did I have to fear? "I love listening to you tell stories. Especially when they're about me."

The girl smiled. "I know all of the stories."

"Tell me one! Right now." Call me a prideful creature, but I never tired of hearing winsome fantasies which starred myself and my new name.

The girl adjusted her long sleeves, which were ill-suited for the summer warmth, but perhaps she had delicate female sensibilities. "All right. Can I be in this one, too?"

"I don't see why not."

The very prospect filled her with enough exhilaration that I could last a week off her pure jubilation alone.

"Once upon a time," she began, her voice breathless. "There was a little boy who refused to grow up."

I puffed out my adolescent chest.

"Every night, he listened at the window of a house he'd visited before, though . . ." She tilted her head. "I wonder if he remembered."

"I never forget," I assured her.

And it was true. *I* never forgot, even if my host did.

The girl smiled, and I felt the boy's consciousness prick in the back of my mind.

"*Let me take control! I want to hear the story.*"

I'm snatching her tonight, boy. I must remain in control.

He turned sullen. "*You always let me have control when we're here.*"

Leave me be. I'll make sure she stays your friend. Forever.

I shoved him away, tried to lull him back to sleep.

He seemed confused, but I redirected my attention to the girl. I'd already missed several parts of the story, which soured my disposition.

" ... the boy crawled through the window one day to whisk the girl off on untold adventures. 'Where are we off to?' the girl questioned." She paused. Leaned in. I did the same until I could catch a hint of the lavender on her breath. The grandfather clock in the parlor chimed the first bell of midnight. "'*Neverland.*'"

I grinned wolfishly.

She continued. "A place with more magic and Lost Boys than you can ever imagine." The girl grasped my hand, and a thrill coursed through my veins, courtesy of the boy lurking in the back of my mind.

I caught a snippet of his thoughts, "*I like the way she talks about me. She thinks I can be better than I am. She tells me so in her stories.*"

I almost snorted, but I didn't want to answer any pesky questions from a nosy girl. *Such adult thoughts from a boy who won't grow up.*

I'd missed another bit of the story, but it seemed the girl was only describing Neverland in great detail. It wasn't until she brought the tale back to me that I paid attention again.

"But what the boy didn't know was that the girl knew the truth."

I straightened. "The truth?"

"From a young age, the girl was obsessed with Neverland. She would tell her brothers the stories that she heard, and they believed, too."

Her brothers? Ah, yes. I combed through my memories until I vaguely remembered some boys that used to flock around her. But, really—they had been minor, unimportant players, and I often rested when my host was here. I scarcely remembered how many existed. Two? Seven? I couldn't say. After all, *they* hadn't woven stories of my greatness.

"And one day, one of the children got taken to Neverland."

I blinked. No—I hadn't. I hadn't taken anyone from this house, had I?

Unless.

Unless my host had.

Any mortal might have blanched, but I kept my bravado. There was nothing too accusatory in what she had said.

Except I noticed her grip on my hand was tighter, and her emotions subtly shifted to a bitter taste.

"Nicholas, the oldest boy, was whisked off to Neverland, while the girl, only ten at the time, hid under the bedsheets, unnoticed. But she heard everything and wanted to go, too." Her voice turned savage as she leaned on her knees to take the higher ground. "She followed. There was no pixie dust, no flying. No second star to the right—those were nothing but fanciful myths to make children more compliant. But in truth, Nicholas, the sister, and the boy from Neverland merely climbed out the window and walked away."

I stood up and stretched to my host's full height. My influence had stunted his aging, so while I should have towered over the girl, I did not. We met eye to eye, hand still locked, all semblances of friendliness gone.

"The boy led Nicholas to a forest, not knowing the little imp of a sister crept behind. And there she saw *it* happen."

She advanced on me, and I attempted to wrest myself away as I growled, "Enough games. I'm done with this."

"*You* may be. But *I* am not."

A sudden influx of pain made me aware of my wrist. I howled and dropped to my knees. A band slid from her arm onto mine, her name engraved in the silver. She shoved me to my knees, a fireplace at my back, the burning metal on my wrist.

Sweat beaded down my face and back.

"Are you scared?" I hissed. I was cold, I was hunger, I was death— this little one should have quivered in her nightgown at my very presence.

But the fire in her eyes rivaled anything in the hearth behind me.

"Not anymore." She squeezed my hand until I wondered if it might break. "I've trained and searched for you for two years. I'm ready."

With my free hand, I tried to push the bracelet back on her. But the very touch of it made me jerk away, uttering words unfit for a nursery.

The story continued. "The girl saw the boy she idolized from the nursery tales shudder. She saw his shadow grow, stretch, and possess its host, like a grotesque puppeteer.

"'What did you do?' the shadow asked with the mouth of the boy—but gone was the youthful, innocent voice with the hint of loneliness. The voice that craved friendship and connection.

"There was no answer that the girl could hear, but she watched as Nicholas backed away. Perhaps he would have fled, and the siblings could have escaped back to the nursery and pretended that it was all just a terrible nightmare, that Neverland still existed in their dreams."

I hissed. I could recall the next part of the story. It had seemed so trivial at the time, a mere hiccup in my master plan.

The girl's eyes sparked and reflected the firelight as she continued. "'How old are you?' the shadow snarled.

"'Fourteen,' Nicholas replied.

"The shadow cursed. 'Too old. You're past your prime.'

"'My prime?' Nicholas asked."

Despite the pain in my arm and the heat on my back, I grinned. A droplet of sweat threaded past my upturned lips as I said, "Would it unnerve you to know the truth? That once a child passes the threshold into adolescence, they never quite have the same flavor as their youth? Or that I can still taste the flesh of everyone I consume?"

The girl flinched.

"Perhaps," she admitted. "Although, it's quite funny—once you witness someone cannibalize your brother, nothing else ever really seems quite as fearsome."

I sniffed the air. No. I didn't smell fear. Just pure, unabashed hatred mixed with vengeful, bitter glee to make it sweet.

She smiled. "But you do get a single-minded purpose."

And the girl grabbed a fireplace poker and whacked my head.

I cried out, but more so from the fact that it, too, burned my flesh. Silver. How had she convinced her parents to make everything in this blasted room silver?

She reared back, aiming the sharp end of her weapon towards my stomach. I attempted once more to shake off the bracelet as I rolled out of the way. It burned me several more times but finally clattered to the ground. I kicked it out of the way, baring my teeth at her.

"I wonder, does the sister taste like the brother?"

The girl arranged herself into a perfect fencing form; her makeshift blade pointed right at my heart. "Why don't you come take a bite?"

I lunged at her. She shoved me into the fireplace with the blunt end. My back hit the trim, and I heard the fizz of my host's hair as it burned. The acrid smell filled my nostrils, and I jerked away.

The girl fell forward, placing her knee on my stomach while a free hand went to my neck. I snapped at her a few times, but she had positioned me so that there was no way I could turn this pathetic human neck and bite her.

"You'll have to leave him," she hissed. "You'll have to leave his body if you want to escape the pain. I know you can. I've read all about your kind—the *real* you."

She pressed the poker against my chest and shoved my hair closer to the fire.

A bit of frost escaped my host's lips as I wriggled inside him. The girl shoved the silver closer to my skin.

"You really want to face me in my true form?" I choked out.

"I would love to. Leave the human husk behind. Don't lurk in his shadow. *Let him go.*"

I glared at her.

If I stayed in his consciousness and she killed him, I would die, too. If I became his shadow, she'd sever my connection in an instant with her blasted silver. But if I left him completely, I could never re-enter, and my time in this body was over—every hour I'd spent cultivating my name, the stories, Neverland.

Wasted.

"Never," I snarled.

She drew back and bludgeoned my chest with the blunt length of the poker.

"*You're letting me get hurt!*" my host screamed.

We're merely biding our time.

"*Until what?*"

She thrashed me once more, closer to the neck. Blood spurted as the curved point of her weapon sliced my skin. My temper flared, and I yelled, both out loud and to my host, "Until we kill her!"

"*No!*" My host sounded like a tantruming child, and his consciousness attacked mine. It felt like he was pummeling me, throwing himself down on the metaphorical floor of our shared mind and throttling my spirit. "*I won't let you hurt her!*"

As if it's ever bothered you to hurt people before.

The girl squeezed until my vision began to darken. Stupid humans—why did they rely so much on blasted oxygen? Why was I as fragile as my host?

"*I've never hurt anyone! I play with my friends—that's all. It's all pretend.*"

His voice sounded a bit hysterical. I wondered how he remembered it all. He couldn't conjure the actual memories, but did he know something was missing? Did he suspect? I'd toyed with his mind so much, erased so many people; I wasn't exactly sure what he thought of anything.

"*Even the nightmares. They're all pretend. It's all in my imagination.*"

I chuckled. I could taste the blood in the back of my throat. I could hardly see anything.

"*Get out of my head! I don't want you here anymore! In her stories, she said that I didn't have to be bad because you made me do the things. She said that I could be good and get rid of you.*"

I could no longer address him out loud, but I could still direct my thoughts at him, though they grew less coherent as the girl choked me. *You'll be lonely again if you kick me out. You'll change. You'll grow up, that horrid thing.*

"*Better to become the adult I should be than stay the child I always have been.*"

He gave me one more good shove, right as my consciousness was about to fade.

Fine!

If he was so in love with this maniac girl, let her kill him, not me.

An icy wind filled the room as I slithered out of the boy's consciousness and became his shadow instead, a dark wolf against the floor.

I fixed my red eyes on the girl and bared my teeth at her, which I assumed looked truly frightening in the glow of the blasted fireplace.

Frost inched its way up the open nursery window, and snow fell with every ragged breath I took.

"You wanted my true form, girl?"

She released her grip on my unconscious host, who looked pale and pathetic slumped on the ground.

"You'll yearn for the creatures of your nightmares by the time I'm done with you."

"Not likely. This is *my* tale now, and you die in it." The girl smirked. "Wendy Darling—wendigo slayer, rescuer of Peter Pan. It has a nice ring to it, doesn't it?"

Wendy advanced on me, poker at the ready. She swung at the floor and hit my abdomen. I roared, and the snow escalated to a blizzard. My teeth could not penetrate her without fully possessing my host. I could only hope to cause her frostbite or send her into hypothermia before she destroyed me.

"They say that some people have altered fairy tales to make them not quite as scary for young children. That there is always a hidden dark side. Won't it be funny in the future if I say I sewed your shadow back on instead of the truth? That I *murdered* the beast and freed Peter Pan of its influence."

She drove her poker against the wood where I lurked and severed my legs in one fell swoop. I howled as my connection snapped. I felt no pain now that I'd left my feeble host behind, but I'd destroy her for her impudence. No one could steal a name from me and live to tell the tale.

At least I could move freely now. I darted across the walls and out the crack in the door, but Wendy pursued.

Silver trinkets lined the doors and hallways. How had her family not noticed her stockpiling these weapons?

I howled as I brushed against a silver statue of armor which had been pushed up against a door. I could hear a babe whimper inside, and another boy shushed him. I had found her brothers at last, but I couldn't possess them as my new hosts, either, now with their guard in the way.

"Every night I lock them in," Wendy said. I whirled around but found her behind me. "You can't slip under the crack without burning yourself, wendigo."

"Does your family think you're insane?" I growled. "Do they threaten to lock you away in an institution?"

"They'd sooner put up with my peculiarities than lose another child." Wendy's fingers curled around her bludgeon. "After all, my father slept outside in the doghouse for a week straight after Nicholas' death, in some desperate attempt to prevent anyone from kidnapping one of us. My family may be peculiar, but we're loyal."

I swore and tried to slip past Wendy. She swiped at me and tore a large hole in my body.

I heard a man's snore down the opposite end of the hall, but a similar suit of armor blocked my path. Silver bells littered the stairs and banisters, cutting off any escape.

It was just Wendy and me.

The more she sliced at me, the lower the temperature dropped as I unleashed more of my wintery powers. Frost crawled up her arms, ruining any flavor they might have once possessed.

She flexed her arms to keep her elbows limber, taunting me through blue lips.

I blustered and blew; she burned and bruised. Suddenly her unseasonably warm clothes didn't seem quite so ridiculous. Her determination, hot like cider, pained my heart.

I panted, my body riddled with stab wounds, my shadowy form small, my fight all but gone.

And then Wendy Darling, wendigo slayer, drew back and speared me right through the heart.

It took me years to fix myself. That's one thing about wendigos: unless you kill us inside a host's body, we can only be defeated, never slayed.

Our shadows always reform, our wounds always heal. And as I watched the young family traipse through Kensington Gardens, I knew.

One day I would come for them again.

The auburn-haired woman bent down to the young redheaded girl, who wielded a stick. The taller man held a chubby boy in his arms, perhaps too scared to put him in a pram.

Perhaps he still remembered that part of the myth.

The small girl gazed upon the statue of Peter Pan. "Mummy, it *does* look like Daddy!"

Wendy cast her husband a smile over her shoulder. "Do you think so, love?"

Peter turned red. "I don't know. I don't really think I look anything like that."

His voice was much deeper than the host I'd once inhabited. Did I feel some kind of emotion?

Yes.

Bitterness. Rage. *Hatred.*

"Now, let me tell you a story." Wendy picked up a stick. "About Neverland. And shadows, wendigos, and darkness. It's our job to defend the world from these nightmares, my dear. So that all nurseries are filled with sweet dreams and stories."

Wendy picked up a stick and began to gently swat at her daughter's. "Once upon a time, there was a boy named Peter Pan . . . ."

I turned away. The Darlings were preparing for a rematch with me, so it was only fair that I returned the favor.

So, I ask again—what's in a name?

The people who have seen what I am, what I truly am, call me a wendigo. They say the name in fear, lock the doors and bar the windows.

But I will claim a new name.

Start a new legend, and the children will come.

Just as the children of the forest once stumbled into the domain of Baba Yaga.

Just as the Pied Piper once led those beautiful, delicious children out of the town of Hamelin.

Just as they whispered sweet stories in the nurseries, innocent dreams and wishes to have a visit from Peter Pan.

One day I will return.

I will always come to claim my Lost Boys.

The Tale Continues in Volume Two

SHADOWS, DARLING

Anne J. Hill

Sweet girl, close your eyes
Ignore the silhouettes you see
Dancing in your nursery.
Everyone has a shadow
That follows wherever they go.
Sometimes it hides
When faced with the light
But soon it'll be back
To hold your hand.
The light fades, and darkness
Drags the shadow away
Again, forever coming
And going, the shadows
That dance at your side.
In Neverland, shadows
Have a mind of their own.
A hook slashing without a hand

Wings fluttering with no command
Shadowy fins splashing
Boys in trees without the body.
But don't worry, little one.
In London, shadows are
Normal, have no free will.
So don't check under your bed
For monsters in the night
Because these shadows
Don't come for little girls.
Except for maybe the one
Standing in your window
And the one on your wall
The one flying above your face.
But forget them, Wendy
And fly away with me.
I promise I'm safe, sweet
The shadow of Peter Pan.
I'll take you to Neverland
Where little girls fight deadly
Shadows, darling.

BLOOD OF INNOCENCE

Anne J. Hill

SHADOWS WISPED ACROSS London. The moon blazed behind Big Ben, casting silhouettes of death that slithered through the streets. Searching. They sought out the blood of innocence.

A child-like heart. A kind old woman. A bed in a nursery. Innocence.

Stars twinkled in the night sky, promising a world of wonder. A world where nothing could go wrong. Utter bliss. If only he could touch the stars and be swept off his feet.

He leaned out his window and watched the hands on Big Ben *tick tock* the hours away. A breeze swept across his wrinkled cheeks. It reminded him of days when his biggest worries were sneaking out into the garden to chase birds and play with the neighbor girl. They'd climb the big oak tree—she'd pretend it was their home full of children, and he'd pretend it was his camp alone in a magical forest.

But then he grew up, and he married that girl.

He sighed heavily out the window. If only he'd stayed young forever in the garden. Lily was old now too, but unlike him, she'd stayed innocent. Full of life and love. The old age never seemed to bother her, usually.

He ran his fingers through his graying hair. The world looked so peaceful out the window. Except for the shadows that bent and quirked. Most would see a lamppost or a bench thrown to the ground.

But not him.

He saw fangs. Scales. Slithering snakes.

Slimming their way through the darkness. None would come for *him*. Innocence did not live in his heart.

Well.

Not anymore.

"Lily, darling," he whispered into the night air. "I'm sorry, my love." But they were just words.

He closed his eyes and imagined himself back in the garden, petals gliding against his youthful cheeks. The feeling of complete innocence. He wished he could bottle it up and drink it on a rainy day.

And so he did.

Or, he tried to.

He married the girl when they'd grown up, and she brought him youth every day. His bottle of youth.

Until she grew old.

Pan pulled back in from the window and took in the room. The sweet, soft nursery of his childhood. Once a peaceful lullaby, now a portal to death.

The lamp by the bed flickered, casting flashing shadows on the wall. Slithering shadows.

Pan stood to his creaking feet and walked over to the bed that was much too small for the old woman lying in it.

"I'm sorry, darling-dear. It was the only way." He reached out and stroked her crinkled cheeks that had once been so smooth and soft. "You know how the fairies get."

The black snakes that only Pan could see curled around the bedpost. Forked tongues flapping.

Lily didn't respond.

Pan reached down, wrapped his hand around the hilt, and yanked his bloody blade out of her throat. "I'll need this again sometime."

The shadows crawled over her, choking the lingering life from her veins.

"Thank you for keeping my heart young for so long. Don't worry, my tiger. I'll be young again. Thanks to you." He smiled at their favorite pet name. Always spunky and viscous and independently youthful. His Tiger Lily.

Her skin cracked under the weight of the shadows. Slowly fading from this life.

He didn't feel bad for her. Not even when she'd struggled against him—begged him not to. Not even when he saw the horror in her eyes when his blade stabbed her throat. Not even when the blood pooled out of her mouth. Not even now, the bed empty with nothing left but her red stains.

She'd grown up. Gotten boring. Complained about her aches and pains. Reminded him of their age, that they'd someday die, and needed to plan for their children's futures.

But now, thanks to the shadowy fairies, *he* would never die.

Not truly.

Pan ran his finger over the blade and presented it to the slithering fairy at his feet. "I've done it. You owe me my body back."

The snake rose up, tongue flicking, and looked at him with beady eyes. Its fangs extended and sank into Pan's neck. Man and fairy tumbled to the floor. Pan's body writhed in pain. His limbs felt like they were shattering—a broken mirror. His vision blurred until all he could see was dust particles and stars dancing around him.

And then, blackness.

Pan woke, his head pounded, a thousand little knives stabbed into his brain. He blinked but could barely see. He groaned and pushed himself to a sitting position, expecting to be in the nursery.

Pan felt grass under his fingers, and he froze.

Through his ringing ears, he could hear what sounded like waves crashing on sand. A warm breeze washed over him, and birds twittered above.

This was no nursery.

"Hello, Pan," a voice, soft and sweet, spoke in front of him.

He blinked, trying to regain his full sight, and slowly a little girl came into view.

Lily!

Pan rubbed his face and blinked again. There she stood, as young as she'd been when he first met her, hiding behind a bundle of tiger lilies in the garden.

She's not supposed to be here!

She gave him a pure smile.

Pan looked down at his hands. His heart rate picked up. The wrinkles were gone. The ache of old age vanished. The fairies had kept their promise.

He got his body back forever in exchange for the blood of innocence.

"Aren't you happy to see me?" Lily pouted.

Pan looked at her again. "Where are we?"

"Neverland. I've been waiting an awfully long time for you. Almost thought you'd given up on me. What took you so long?"

Pan watched her. He felt nothing but anger. She wasn't supposed to be here. He'd be young forever, without a nagging wife. She may look like the child he once knew, but she was just as old, scolding him like he was late to dinner. He pushed himself to his feet and said, "Neverland?" He brushed his hands off. "You weren't supposed to come with me."

"But aren't you glad I did?" Her eyes grew dark, like shadows in the night.

"No." Pan crossed his arms. "I want you to leave and never come back. This is *my* land. *My* reward. *My* agreement. You didn't earn this like I did."

Earned it with her blood.

"Pan . . ." she whispered. Her face contorted, studying him, as if a memory was coming back to her. Her eyes widened, and she lunged at him. "You killed me!" She clawed at his face. Pan struggled against her until he felt the blade at his side. He grinned and yanked it free. Pan pinned her to the ground and pressed the blade to her throat.

"Let's make one thing clear," Pan growled. "I'm *never* growing old with you again. You stole everything from me. You forced me to grow up and worry about things like taxes and baby diapers and wills and mortgages. Never again. This is *my* story. Not yours. If I ever see you here again, I will kill you. Because this new world is so magical, and I'm feeling generous, I'll let you go this one time. But never again."

Lily's eyes filled with angry tears as she listened. "Pan, please don't leave me, you bastard. Don't you love me?" Her lips trembled.

"You think I still love you?" He smirked. "Well, then. I'll have to leave you with a reminder that I don't." He gripped her arm over her head and stabbed his blade into her wrist. Lily screamed louder than he'd ever heard, but it didn't deter him. He stabbed and sawed and bent her wrist until her hand laid in a puddle of blood, detached from her arm.

Tears soaked her plump cheeks, her body frozen in shock. The same look of horror he saw when he killed her in the nursery coated her face.

And Pan felt nothing.

He picked himself up and stashed his blade away. "If you want to live, you better tend to all that blood."

And then he left her, alone, in the middle of the beautiful forest he'd discovered all by himself. She might die, but he didn't really care. He hadn't killed her this time. It'd be her own fault if she didn't find a way to stop the bleeding and attach something else for a hand.

With nothing in his heart, Pan trotted through the forest. The ease of running filled the empty space in his chest with a sort of glee, and he ran faster until he reached a giant hollowed-out oak tree.

He grinned to himself. He'd always wanted to live inside a tree.

The Tale Continues in Volume Two

LOST GIRL

Beka Gremikova

She looks at me, eyes wide—
Beseeching for a kiss.
I have seen that look so many
times, on every Wendy
who lingers too long.
Why do they always grow up,
Even though they've flown
the coop of the aging world?
Is Never-land broken? Is its magic dead?
Or am I the only one who believes
Enough to keep this youthful frame?

She steps closer, lips puckered,
Eyes gleaming, yearning.
I have seen that look so many times,
on every Wendy who thinks
She can change

the never-ending
Never-land.
I sigh. Always, they age. Always,
they break.
How useless.
It is time to start anew.
I slip my dagger from its sheath
And step forward to meet
Her kiss
with
a killing blow.

'TIL SOMEONE LOSES A HAND

Lara E. Madden

THE JOLLY ROGER rose and fell rhythmically on the waves. Sirens splashed alongside its hull and waved to the crew with sharp-toothed grins. The captain shuddered when one met his eye. His withered hand traveled to his chest, feeling the ancient scars left on him by a siren's talons when he was a boy. It had been many years since he'd been in Neverland.

There was a twisted nostalgia about the island. It lingered on the breeze. Salty mist and the damp smell of fresh rainforest foliage, but also a sweeter scent that he couldn't quite place. Something like licorice or... The captain shook his head. Pixie dust. That was it. Few people knew that pixie dust had a smell: sweet and faint but very distinct. He wasn't sure if he cherished the scent or abhorred it. The ancient emotions had been tangled together so long, the love and the loathing for this place called Neverland, that he doubted they could ever be separated. Anyway, death was drawing too close to him now. He doubted he had enough time left to sort it out.

Time...

A heavy wave rocked the ship, and the captain clamped his hook onto the banister to regain balance. He leaned against the railing to scan the shoreline. Once, he had known every square foot of the island so intimately that he could travel through it in his dreams. For years after his return to the real world, he continued to revisit Neverland in his mind. But the past had begun to fade decades ago. He had only the vague shapes of memories now, and he would often feel their edges like a blind man studying a statue, trying to remember what it looked like.

"Thank you for bringing me here, Tinkerbell," he said quietly. A small glowing orb settled on his shoulder, speaking to him with a tiny ringing sound. When she appeared to him a few weeks earlier, he'd been surprised to find that he could still understand her language. She offered him a second chance at the life he had squandered. He still hardly believed it was possible, but here they were, on a journey through time and space to the place that always felt most like home.

Being in Neverland caused everything to rush back to him. He recalled the places he'd run as a boy, the peaks he'd conquered. The shortcuts and vantage points, the favorite spots for an ambush. He knew, as the ship steered by a sharp rock overhang, that they were going directly under one of these ambush points, and his rival wouldn't be able to resist such an opportunity.

The crew of the Jolly Roger totaled eight besides the captain. All had their eyes on the island, their senses attuned to notice any movement or shifting shadow. Tinkerbell fluttered away from the captain's shoulder and disappeared into a coil of rope. There was a tense, quiet moment as everyone waited for the attack. The captain glanced at the sky, brought his good hand to his forehead to block out the sun, and—

"*Whoooooooop,*" came the war cry from above. The captain ducked and swung his hook in the same instant, but the flying boy swooped down and missed him by only inches. Flashes of green cloth and red hair were visible as the boy dodged between masts and weaved behind sails. The sun glinted off of his sword as he swung it haphazardly. Then, once he'd grown bored of his own theatrics, the boy perched himself on the ledge of the crow's nest and lifted the sword over his head.

"Haven't seen you around here before," the boy shouted down. "Well, I thought you should know whose island you've stumbled upon." He placed his fists on his hips and puffed out his chest. "I am Peter Pan, and I am the king of this land, which makes me the sovereign over this ship and your crew." The boy dive-bombed the crew again, coming so close that several sailors dropped to their bellies. He spun a few circles above the captain's head, just out of reach. "What should I call you?" he said. "Hmmm… Hooky? Hookster? Hook-Hand? How about… Captain Hook!"

The captain gritted his teeth. He looked down at the stump where his right hand used to be. The disfigurement that marked the worst day of his life trivialized in a nickname. *Captain Hook.*

"Come down here and speak with me like a man," the captain shouted at the sky as Pan danced above their heads.

"'Fraid I can't do that, Hook." The boy laughed. "I'd be breaking the first law of Neverland: never do *anything* like a man!" Pan darted toward the deck to hover just above their heads, only a foot or so out of reach. The seven-foot-tall shipmate jumped up to snag him, but Pan dodged him easily and knocked the man's head with the hilt of his sword. He crossed his arms in vain triumph and stared down at the captain. "And that means, sadly, you'll have to go. You and all your crew."

The captain rolled his eyes and growled back, "I know the law of Neverland, boy. I wrote the damn thing."

Pan's features flashed confusion for a brief moment, and he dropped a few inches. Just close enough for the furious shipmate to grab an ankle and drag him toward the deck. The other crew members dove on him. Pan swung his sword and made contact with one sailer's arm, who screamed but managed to get the boy's wrist in a vise grip until the sword clattered on the wooden floor. A third member came with rope to tie his arms and legs, but it took all of the sailors to pin Pan down before they could secure him. Even then, he managed a few times to break one of his hands free and land a punch. They worked swiftly while Pan squirmed and cursed and railed.

"You won't keep me here for long," he screamed. "The Lost Boys will come for me any minute."

The Lost Boys... The mention stole the wind from the captain's lungs. He turned away before Pan could see his face fall. The Lost Boys were still alive. In this world, in this timeline, they still ran through the forest. They were vibrant, strong, well, and real. His hand fiddled with the leather straps of his hook. He might still have time to make things right.

"Check him for weapons," the captain said as the crew secured Pan to the mast. "He won't just have a sword; he keeps a knife strapped to his belt and another on a chain around his neck. Check his pockets, too. He'll have a pouch of pixie dust or a potion for emergencies."

"Sir," one of the men said to him privately. "You told us not to hurt any of them. What will we do if the others come?"

"Then we'll let him go."

"But what if this is our only chance?"

The captain shook his head and clapped a hand on the man's shoulder. "We can't force him to do anything. We'll try to make him see reason. There will be no battle."

He couldn't be responsible for the deaths of the Lost Boys. Not again. And if one of his crew would be harmed because they came on this mission with him, he would never forgive himself.

He patted the man's shoulder and looked past him toward the mast. Pan screamed profanities and pulled violently against his binds. The captain strode toward him with footsteps that commanded authority. He spoke with a gravelly voice, roughened by age and a lifetime of smoking a tobacco pipe. "Peter Pan." He leveled his gaze at the boy and waited for him to meet his eye.

Pan shot him a glare, and the captain had a clear view of his features for the first time. He tried not to let the boy see his shock, but *that face*. It was like looking in a pool of clear water years ago. He cleared his throat.

"My name is—"

"Your name is Hook!" Pan shot back. He snorted loudly and spat at the captain. The old man sighed and wiped the spit from his cheek with a handkerchief.

"My *name*," he continued calmly, enunciating each word, "is Peter Rogers." He watched as the color drained from Pan's face. There. He had his attention. "I was born in London, in 1897. I spent my first years in a poorhouse, though I told a group of Lost Boys that I was the child of an overbearing mother and father who I'd run away from."

Confusion and horror etched into the lines of Pan's face. "What sort of sick joke is this?" he demanded. "Who are you?"

"I befriended a group of fairies when I was a small child, and they taught me to fly and showed me a land of magic and mystery and danger—"

"Who *are* you?"

"I made myself the boy king of that land and vowed that I would never, ever grow up." His tone intensified with every word. "No matter what, I would never become a man. I surrounded myself with friends who would follow and worship me." Fury and regret mixed together in his core. "I did what I wanted. I cared nothing for the outcomes of my decisions because consequences and responsibilities, and sacrifices were only for adults. I fell in love with a girl named Wendy—" His voice broke on her name.

"You're a liar! You've only come to steal from me, and when the Lost Boys get here, you will suffer for it!"

The captain stared at him sadly and grunted. They were getting nowhere. "You want proof of who I am, Peter?" He opened his ruffled shirt to reveal the jagged scars that ran down his chest. "These are from when a siren attacked me. I know they are familiar to you." He pulled back his left sleeve and nodded toward a similar scar on Pan's bare arm. "This was a knife fight." He pointed toward his leg. "The time Curly dropped a pot of boiling water on my foot. Burned for weeks. And Tinkerbell . . ." The captain glanced around. "Where is that fairy anyway?"

Tinkerbell flew out from her hiding place and landed on the captain's shoulder. Pan studied the captain's face until recognition flickered in his eyes. His breathing sharpened, and his mouth turned down in a horrified scowl.

"Peter," the captain straightened his spine to stand at his full height. "You know the truth. I am your future. I've come to warn you."

The Tale Continues in Volume Two

CAPTAIN

Anne J. Hill

Water splashes against the bows
Of this old ship of mine
I am her captain
And this is my crew
Lost souls looking for a home
Always young at heart
And always young by skin
We'll sail across the sea
With Hook at our tail
Hunting down this ship
But I am her captain
And this is *my* crew
A family like no other
With fairy dust in our eyes
And daggers at our sides
Yo ho, yo ho
I am the captain

And this is *my* crew
Sailing the ocean blue
To plunder and loot
No one will stop me
No one will stop us
Because
I am the captain
And this is my ship
—and my faithful crew

The Tale Continues in Volume Two

PLENUS LUNA

Maseeha Seedat

ET ME MAKE one thing clear: there is no Neverland. Well, not the Neverland you grew up fantasizing over. There never was, and there never will be. The idea of a magical, *whimsical* Neverland was cooked up by you dim-witted humans to ease your darling children's nightmares, to ensure they slept peacefully through the night so you could too.

Well, I hate to break it to you, but my island is far from your daydreams.

That's why it's called Neverland. Once you get there, you never return.

"Pan! Pan, wake up."

My eyes fluttered open. I strained to see the figure at the edge of my mattress through the darkness. Darkness. I turned to face the window. It was pitch black outside. Why was someone waking me up in the *middle of the night*?

Footsteps shuffled across the dirt floor. I closed my fingers over the dagger under my pillow.

"Pan?" the voice repeated. "Did you hear me? Wake up!"

I knew that voice. Jaime. He would pay for disturbing my sleep.

The footsteps halted near my head. "Pan?"

My arm shot up, throwing my blanket in his face. He lurched backward, blinded as I leaped off the bed. I shoved my elbow into his stomach. My shadow would have copied me if it wasn't so dark.

Jaime flopped onto the bed, and I pinned him there, holding the dagger to his throat. His hands struggled under the blanket, soon ripping it off his face. I grabbed a torch from my pedestal and flicked it on.

I grinned. "Gotcha."

Jaime grinned back, curly black locks falling over his face. "I can see that. Why, though, I can't understand."

"You woke me up." I stuffed my dagger into my belt, mimicking his squeaky voice. "*Why, though, I can't understand.*"

"It's the last full moon of summer. Don't tell me you forgot our tradition."

Oh right. Jaime and I had celebrated Plenus Luna together since we met, voyaging to Skull Rock to remember the year we lived, the creatures we survived—to mark the last good day of the year.

After that... the winter monsters came out, far more fearsome than the beasts of the warmer months. In summer, we could still go stargazing, still wander along the forest paths without fearing for our lives. In fall, there was still the rare chance of visiting the healers' camp and making it home intact. But in winter... setting one foot outside your door meant you'd be walking with a peg leg for the rest of your life.

"Come on!" Jaime yelled.

He ran out the door, knowing I would follow him sooner or later. I quickly yanked my hat onto my head and straightened the red feather on its side as I bolted after him. My feet drummed like thunder against the earth, swirling a dust cloud around me—natural camouflage against the monsters.

I caught up to Jaime at the Hangman's Tree, where he sat on one of its gnarled roots. The naked branches creaked in the breeze, their eerie voices echoing in the silence. Goosebumps pricked along my arms. Two crows cried overhead as the clouds parted to reveal the moon, its beams kind enough to grant my shadow a weak lifeline. It danced at my toes, pulling me toward the coast.

I knew why.

Skull Rock. Time for our tradition to commence.

"What are you waiting for?" Jaime scowled. "The moonlight won't last all night."

I tore my eyes away from my lively shadow. "I'm waiting for you to catch up."

With that, I took off, my shadow racing alongside me. Jaime hollered behind me but soon caught up. We dashed through the night, over hills and into valleys, our manic footsteps kicking the sweet fragrance of cosmos and lilies into the empty night sky. It wouldn't be empty for long; Jaime and I both knew that. And we were ready.

After climbing the third hill, we met our first monster. A fae with wings of smoke descended from the wispy clouds, her pale skin covered in scars, typical for a life on Neverland. We called her Tink for the metallic clanking of her silver heart, a common trait among the fae, granting them the ability to move and think faster than any other creature on the island. *So what?* She was still flesh-and-bone. Jaime and I could outwit a fae any time of the year.

Now the fae believed in three things: faith, trust, and pixie dust.

Tink only believed in one.

She twirled her gloved fingers, summoning a cloud of glittering pixie dust into her palm.

"Cover your eyes!" Jaime yelled as Tink blew the specks into the air.

The wind shifted, almost on cue, and I shielded my eyes as the dust drifted toward us. The searing pain of Tink's mischief was something I *definitely* didn't want to experience again.

"Down the hill!" Jaime ordered.

He skidded down the dew-soaked grass into the valley below. I followed him, and Tink followed me, her wings hissing with every beat. She never could resist a good chase. It was too bad she had fallen for our trap.

Down in the valley, the towering hills blocked the breeze, leaving Tink only her delicate fairy breath to carry her weapon. Without the wind, she was almost powerless. And she knew that.

Tink twirled her fingers again, summoning more dust to overcome our trick.

I glanced at Jaime. He nodded.

We charged at Tink and tackled her by the legs. A grunt escaped her as she stumbled, flicking her open palm into the air. Jaime and I each grabbed an arm and a leg, holding her firmly to the ground. She squirmed as the dust settled on her bare skin.

Tink's scream echoed mercilessly, reverberating off the hills as she writhed in agony. Swamp-green boils bubbled and burst over her skin, spewing puss like geysers. The scars would never fade.

We left her there as the acid burned the grass beneath her. She wouldn't come after us for a few weeks at least; Jaime and I had timed it before. Tink wouldn't dare to attack us until her wounds healed. We scaled the hill again and didn't stop running until we reached the coast of Neverland.

That was where we encountered our second lot of beasts: the mermaids.

These were not the mermaids of your fairytales. Oh no, these mermaids were not from *your* Neverland. They didn't spend their days in crystal-clear lagoons, chattering on the rocks or swimming under roaring waterfalls. They were from my Neverland, and they suited that description just fine, residing in the ocean depths far from the rest of us.

Well, until they were hungry.

"Oh, Pan . . ." sang one of the monsters, her wholly-white eyes watching me closely. "Don't you want to come for a swim?"

"No thanks," I said, scurrying across the sandy beach to where our canoe was hidden under a pile of driftwood and palm fronds. "I'd rather drown."

"That can be arranged," said another, dragging her fishtail through the shallows, ocean waves lapping against her pale, slimy body.

Jaime started to offload the driftwood, throwing each log over his shoulder to scare the mermaids. It didn't work. I swung a palm frond wildly, forcing the beasts away from our only escape to Skull Rock. Jaime lifted a log over his head, ready to hurl it, but it was too heavy.

He stumbled into the crashing waves on the shore.

A mermaid grabbed his ankle. He growled as her claws sank into his skin, blood staining the beach red, her venom racing through his veins.

"You're both targeting the wrong boy," she said, and I knew her voice. It had haunted my sleep long enough for me to remember it. She was the most cunning of the pod: Hannan.

Her nose flared, sniffing out our emotions as her pointed ears twitched at the drum of our heartbeats. "Ah yes, this boy... Jaime, ah yes, Jaime... he has been through so much, and at such a young age."

"Don't listen to her!" I said, yanking the wood off our canoe. I threw a piece at Hannan's head. She dodged it easily.

"First, his brothers, the Lost Boys, all taken in the middle of the night," she whispered as Jaime's veins turned black. It wouldn't be long before he gave in. "Then his father, murdered by a pirate at sea, then his mother killed by the grief that consumed her."

Jaime's fist trembled furiously, and he bit his lip to hold in tears. Hannan cackled with glee.

"Oh yes, I know my child. I know your suffering, your anger, your hatred and despair. I know how you wandered this merciless island until you met a boy just as lost as you." The beast shot me a dark glare before turning back to her prey. "He didn't help you find your way. But *I* can. Let me help you. Let me take it all away."

"Jaime, don't do it!" Tears stung my eyes, threatening to block my vision. I couldn't break, not yet, not until Jaime was safe.

I shoved the canoe into the fizzing water and pulled out my dagger. Jaime blinked back tears, taking a step further into the ocean.

"Please," he whimpered, "take it all. Take it all away."

Another step. Another cackle from Hannan.

"Oh no, you don't." I turned to my shadow. "Get rid of the beast."

My shadow rolled up his sleeves, his opaque face parting in a sly grin. He leaped across the sand, consuming Hannan's tail in a fistful of darkness. She screeched and squirmed as her sisters raced to her aid. But she never let go of Jaime.

A shadow-dagger sprung from my clone's waist. He hurled himself at the slimy creatures, holding them at bay. I grabbed Jaime's arm and ripped Hannan's claw from his leg.

"What are you doing?" Jaime hissed. "Let go of me! I'm going with the mermaids."

"Not on my watch." I bandaged the wound with my green hat to slow the bleeding. "Now, hold still."

I picked up his squirming body, my shadow hoisting Jaime's legs out of the beasts' reach.

"No!" Jaime screamed. The mermaids echoed his cry as they clawed their way to the canoe.

"It was nice seeing you, Hannan," I wheezed, "but we've got places to be. See you next summer!"

I hurled Jaime into the boat. His head bashed against the seat, and he flopped unconscious. Oh well. *It's better than him screaming his lungs out.* I scrambled for the oars, and we took off, my arms whirling faster than they had in my life. The mermaids were soon moonlit specks on the horizon.

I allowed myself a short sigh of relief.

They wouldn't follow us. No, they wouldn't dare. Not with Tick Tock slumbering far below in eternal darkness. No one would follow us out here, not now.

We were safe, at least for the moment.

Eventually, I stopped rowing, turning to face Skull Rock. The mountain's silhouette lingered in the distance, the wind howling through its open jaw, beckoning us to join it on the last full moon of summer. We would be there within the hour, that was if Jaime lived to see it.

He had to.

"Jaime?" I whispered, leaning over his still body as I swallowed the lump in my throat. "Jaime, can you hear me?"

One blood-shot eye flickered open, then the other. I reached for the lantern beside him with trembling fingers—the one we kept in the boat to ward off Tick Tock—and set the wick burning with a match from my pocket. The flame lit up the dark veins streaking across his pale face. He grinned, revealing a gap between his two front teeth.

"Can you hear me?" I said. A tear dripped to my chin. He had to be all right, *please* ...

Jaime nodded, his eyes rolling in his head. Had Hannan's venom worked its magic already?

It was time to test his memory.

"Tell me the story." I pulled him into a sitting position, forcing my heart to *stop* pounding. "Tell me the story of my shadow." His head dropped forward. I thrust it up firmly. "*Tell me.*"

Jaime cocked his head to the side, then murmured the tale I knew all too well.

"When you were little, not even strong enough to stand on your own two feet, you were struck by the Never Bird. The Never Bird was a small creature, struggling as it flew, like a thin piece of parchment against the wind. One day, it bit you right there." Jaime pointed to the hollow of my right foot, where a deep red scar still remained. "And its venom crept through your veins, killing you from the inside-out. So your parents called the healer Tiger Lily, hoping against all odds that she could save you."

"And what did Tiger Lily do?" I asked. A shiver crept through me as the wind took a sharp turn. Our boat rocked a little, scattering ripples across the ocean.

"Tiger Lily ..." Jaime's voice wandered.

"Focus!"

"Tiger Lily!" His eyes shot wide open. "The healer cast a fearful charm that dragged the illness out of you by your little toe. But you were a horrible child." Jaime laughed to himself, the color returning to his cheeks. His veins began to fade back to normal. "You struggled and squirmed, weakening her spells. At the end of the day, she saved your life, but the venom's darkness is still tethered to you, forming a mischievous shadow with its own mind. You will never escape it."

My chest heaved as I exhaled. Jaime was still in his right senses. He was probably just in shock from Hannan's tricks.

Something plopped in the ocean a few feet from us. I swung the lantern around, illuminating the hushed ripples of the ever-moving ocean.

Could it be Tick Tock? The beast was terrified of light, the hope it carried. He wouldn't dare to come near us.

Another plop. This time behind me.

My fingers tightened over my dagger.

"Jaime, how strong are you?"

"Stronger than you," he smirked, still half-dazed.

"Good." My breathing quickened, my heartbeat a war drum in my ears. "You better start rowing."

Jaime snapped to life, arms pumping as he propelled us toward Skull Rock, his gaze steady to Neverland's shore. I balanced at the bow of the boat, studying the water for any sign of movement below us. We were almost at Skull Rock. We were almost safe. Tick Tock would never come after us. We had a light. He wouldn't come. He wouldn't—

A fountain of water spurted in my face, the frigid sea spray drenching me to the core. Our lantern fizzled out and died. Only the moon's pale face was left to light the way through Skull Rock's towering shadow.

"Pan?" Jaime called out, his back to me. "You alive?"

"Yeah, you?"

"What do you think?"

I wiped my face dry, twirling my dagger over in my fingers. That's when I heard it.

Tick tock....

Tick tock....

My blood turned to ice.

"Keep rowing!" I ordered, almost losing my balance as Jaime took up the oars again.

The first thing I saw was the beast's scales peeking out of the water like a hundred gleaming blades in the moonlight. Then came his tail swinging back and forth to the ticking rhythm in his throat.

"Pan... you're quiet," Jaime said. "What do you see?"

"Just keep rowing!"

I screamed as the beast surfaced, snapping its enormous jaw in my face. My dagger fell from my fingers, landing somewhere at the bottom of the boat.

Jaime whirled around as I teetered and crashed into him. We tumbled off the seat as Tick Tock clamped his teeth over our little rowboat. The wood creaked and snapped, leaving us without a bow.

"You scream like a girl," Jaime scoffed, shoving me off his chest.

"Try telling that to the croc. Maybe he doesn't eat little girls."

Jaime reached for the oars, sweat glistening off his forehead. He cursed as his hands clamped over thin air and Tick Tock yanked the oars into the water. The splintering fibres echoed in the silent night as the crocodile devoured his toothpicks. We were next on the menu.

"You got a plan?" I asked, watching the beast circle us, my brain consumed with the endless ticking.

"I'm working on it."

Then Tick Tock disappeared, his enormous figure vanishing into the depths. A flurry of bubbles raced to the surface where the beast had been seconds before. I craned my neck over the edge, searching the darkness. Nothing.

Did he just give up?

"See?" I forced a laugh. "That was a breeze."

"I don't like breezes," Jaime snarled, pushing his curls out of his face. "They mess up my hair."

My grin faded as something thumped under our boat.

No....

Thump. It couldn't be.

Thump. But only one beast had that kind of strength.

"Jaim—"

My voice died as Tick Tock raced to the surface, his snout colliding with the bottom of our boat. The force launched us skyward, and we flew from our seats only to plummet into the freezing ocean.

I burst through the tumbling waves, the saltwater burning my lungs. My heart hammered in my ears as I scanned the water for Jaime. I couldn't see a thing in Skull Rock's shadow.

"Jaime!" I heaved the canoe right-side-up, my shadow lending a helping hand. "Jaime!"

I clambered into the boat, shivering uncontrollably.

"Pan!"

Jaime's head burst through the waves, his long curly hair over his eyes. I bolted toward him, almost flipping the boat again as I sunk my hands into the ice-cold water, paddling as fast as I could.

My life depended on it.

Without Jaime, it wouldn't be one worth living.

"Don't just stand there; help me," I ordered my shadow.

But the clouds drifted over the moon.

My shadow died, leaving me alone.

Well, not alone.

Tick Tock was hurtling toward the boat at full speed.

"Pan!" Jaime yelled.

"Give me your hand!" I reached for Jaime as he swam closer. He stretched out to me, fingers splayed. Almost... Almost...

Tick Tock lurched out of the water right between Jaime and me. I pulled my hand to my chest, the boat rocking maniacally. Jaime didn't have the same fortune.

The crocodile clamped his jaw over Jaime's wrist, consuming it all—fingers, nail and bone—leaving him with a stump of spurting blood.

His scream echoed in the silence.

Tears coursed down to my chin, and I didn't bother wiping them away.

The clouds parted, bringing my shadow back to life.

"Oh, *now* you come." I couldn't help rolling my eyes. "Help me save him!"

My shadow nodded eagerly. It dove into the ocean and held the boat by the stern. Its legs kicked furiously, propelling us through the water.

But it steered in the wrong direction.

No. My shadow had its focus set on Neverland's coast, on home and the safety of my bed. It didn't care. *Why didn't it care about Jaime?*

I flickered my gaze over the boat in search of my knife, hoping beyond hope to use it and scare my shadow. It was nowhere in sight.

It must have fallen into the water when Tick Tock attacked.

"Swim, Jaime!" I hollered as the wind returned. "Swim, and I'll pull you out."

Jaime's head sunk beneath the waves, the water blood-red in the moonlight.

No...

My heart drummed faster.

"Turn us around," I commanded. My shadow refused. "Turn us around!" I grabbed the wispy black trail at my feet, desperate to pull my stupid, self-preserving shadow out of the water so it would *stop swimming.* If only I could find my blasted dagger.

"Jaime!" Tears streamed down my face.

Jaime was right. I *did* scream like a little girl.

It wasn't long before I was back on Neverland.

I ducked below the waves, blinking through the murkiness as Pan's boat faded away. I didn't even scream after him. What was the use? He had abandoned me. He wouldn't save me.

It was up to me to save myself now.

My heart pounded like a war drum as I raced to Skull Rock. It was only a couple hundred feet away, a distance I could swim with ease if I wasn't cold and bleeding and missing a hand.

Oh. And being chased by a crocodile.

Why did I have to be so delicious?

I surfaced to scan the water. Dark scales loomed in the distance, growing closer with every shaky breath I took. I forced myself to think back to the memories of my home, my home before Pan. What were my father's rules on surviving this brute while sailing Neverland's murky waters?

The scales were close now, each at least the size of my head. Time was up. I took one last breath before sinking into the waves, Pan's dagger gripped in my good hand. It was a good thing I had picked it up before that two-faced traitor did.

A dark mass filled my vision, blood-stained teeth glinting in the moonlight as I suddenly remembered my father's warning.

His senses are weak, escape from the jaws is bleak, after the death roll is the best time to retreat.

The beast's enormous, yellow eyes came into view, and I was ready.

He clamped his jaws over the stump of my arm...but he didn't bite. No, Tick Tock was going to whirl me around in a death roll until I was streamlined, easy enough to swallow in one gulp.

How stupid.

My arm had barely been a snack. I wouldn't let him have another bite.

And that mission wouldn't be painless. The agony coursed through my body, sending bubbles to the surface as I screamed. *Focus.* I couldn't give in, not now. As spasms exploded up my arm, I stabbed Pan's blade into the monster's eye over and over. He gurgled as a dark liquid seeped down his scaly face.

But he didn't let go.

The beast spun around in a death roll, a movement used to position his prey in line with his throat, or so my father said. I didn't struggle, instead spun in the same direction as Tick Tock, waiting for him to exhaust himself.

I hoped my breath would last the fight.

Black spots clouded my vision as the creature *finally* slowed down. I shook my head vigorously, reaching to skewer his eyes, his ears, his nostrils. Anything to disorientate him further.

His jaw loosened.

I yanked myself free, rushing to the surface. My breath sputtered out of my aching chest, and I couldn't help the smile on my lips. I had survived. I was probably the first since my father had faced Tick Tock all those years ago. Sure, I was bleeding, tired and scraped all over from Tick Tock's teeth, but I was alive.

But now was not the time to celebrate.

I gripped the dagger firmly and began the journey to Skull Rock, the moonlight guiding me as I left Tick Tock far behind.

I dragged my aching body onto the pebble shore of Skull Rock, the stones ripping through my skin. I didn't care. If I didn't get my stump fixed soon, I would bleed to death.

"Pan, you traitor!" I screamed until my throat burned. Hot tears poured down my face as the salt water stung my wounds. "I thought you had my back! I trusted you. How dare you leave me to die!"

My gaze dropped to where Hannan had poisoned me, staring at Pan's hat wrapped over the wound. I untied it and lobbed it into the waves.

The bleeding down there had stopped anyway.

I pulled my shirt over my head and ripped it in two, clamping the stump with one half, and using my teeth to tourniquet my forearm with the other. The fabric was soon red with blood.

"You'll pay for this, Pan!" I turned my glare back to the island. "I swear on the evils of Neverland, I will make you pay, even if it takes me a lifetime—"

My voice cut off, raw from the seawater and my threats.

A sharp pang raced down to my fingers, well, where they used to be. I had to fix my arm, *now*.

I crawled through one of Skull Rock's nostrils into a cavern illuminated by the gentle hue of glow worms: our hideout. It was mine now. Pan didn't deserve it.

Near the nostril was a little fire pit in a ring of ash-stained stones, a crate next to it filled with driftwood from last year. I placed a few twigs in the pit as kindling and dug around for the flint and steel, finding them buried near the crate.

I angled the flint over the kindling so I could strike it with my only hand.

The scrape of metal against rock echoed in the nostril.

"Come on," I whispered, gritting my teeth. I struck it again, harder. A spark. "Please work…." Again. More sparks. The searing agony in my arm intensified. One last time… Red-hot sparks…

Then the twigs caught fire.

I blew on them gently, coaxing the flames to burst into life. They sputtered, flickering meekly. More wood, each piece larger than the last.

And then there was fire.

I held Pan's blade over the flames, wincing as I tore the fabric shred off my stump. It clung to my bloody limb, each tug ripping into me like a Never Bird bite.

The blade was soon blazing red. I tore a strip from my shorts, clamping my jaw over the ball of fabric… and placed the burning metal on my stump.

Oh my stars!

The fabric muffled my cries, tears streaking down my face and sizzling in the flames as I lifted the knife, then put it back, repeating the action to seal the blood vessels but keep the rest of my arm unharmed.

I roared in pain, dislodging the cloth ball. I hadn't expected it to be this bad. And it was Pan's fault. He was to blame for this. He would *pay* for this.

The thought of his arrogant grin filled my mind, somehow numbing the torture I had to endure. I glanced down at the dark, bloody mess I made. But my arm wasn't dripping. It was sealed. I quickly grabbed a spare shirt from another crate, swinging it over my head and arm to form a sling.

Unless I was infected, I had a pretty good chance for survival.

I let my gaze wander across the cavern, the memories etched into every crevice, every stone on the ground. The crackling fire filled my ears as I thought over the first step of my revenge.

I would continue our tradition without him. That would teach him a lesson.

My body trembled from the chilled wind as I stumbled to the back of the nostril. The fingers of my good hand ran over the ivory stone of Skull Rock. *Where is it? Where is it?* My hand found a set of lines carved into the rock. I picked up a pebble, etching in a few new lines.

One for the year we—no, *I,* had survived on Neverland. Nineteen for the number of monsters *I* had encountered, bringing my kill count up to two hundred. A milestone we were meant to celebrate tonight. Together.

Never again.

"To another winter," I whispered, "and another summer when the snow melts. To more walks in the moonlight and more wins against the cards we've been dealt. To another year, and another Plenus Luna: the last full moon of summer."

"Ho there!"

I whirled around, wiping away my tears. There was a boat on shore. A little rowboat. It couldn't be… Pan?

"Who's there?" I asked, rising to my trembling feet.

"My name is Smee." A short, tubby silhouette rose out of the boat. An adult? I hadn't seen one of them in years. "I heard you screaming—"

"I don't scream. Only little girls scream."

"My mistake." I could hear the smile in his voice. "I heard you *yelling.* Are you all right?"

I ducked out of the nostril, marching forward to stand face-to-face with this stranger. "I'm *fine*," I growled through gritted teeth.

"But your hand is gone."

"Look, I don't need your help or your pity. I don't need anyone. I can survive by myself."

Smee faltered back a bit. He straightened, pushing his half-moon glasses back up his nose. "Oh, I don't doubt that. You're a very strong young man. But you don't have the tools to save yourself. I do. Let me check your arm, make sure there's no infection; then you can go. No favors, no catch. All right?"

I peered over his shoulder. His boat was empty. "Where are your tools?"

Smee pointed behind him to a ship far off in the ocean, a little speck in the distance. "They're over there. We won't harm you, I promise."

We? He wasn't working alone. "I don't trust you." I crossed my good arm over the make-shift sling.

"Then take this." Smee loosened the scabbard at his side, handing his sword to me. I couldn't help my gasp. Compared to the crude weapons Pan and I used to build ... this was a masterpiece. "It's the only one I have. I can't harm you without it."

I looked at the sword, then at Smee, then at my stump. I needed the help *desperately*. It seemed I would have to play along for now.

"Fine, you have yourself a deal."

Smee grinned, bowing toward me. "Then welcome aboard the Jolly Roger, my friend."

The Tale Continues in Volume Two

TICK TOCK

Anne J. Hill

Tick tock
Goes the clock
The one in the tower
Tracking the time we age
Forever heading for adulthood
And all the grown-up responsibilities
If only we could stop the clock
Or better yet, capture it and
Lock it up in jaws of the
Mighty croc called
Tick Tock

THE DEATH OF PETER PAN

PART ONE

Savanna Roberts

JOHN WANTED TO be a lawyer.

Ever since Father explained the job to him, John had thought of nothing else. He studied justice and government, pondering law in his spare time when he should have been washing the dishes with me. He surpassed his schoolmates. He'd lose Father during some of their in-depth conversations. He wanted to leave London when he was old enough to go to Harvard. He swore day in and day out that the first thing he would do would be to find Jeremy Long's kidnapper and put him behind bars. The kidnappers would rue the day they stole a boy from his bed and devastated an entire family.

Michael was too young to have a career in mind. He had only just started primary school. But he had a want all his own that he whispered to me every bedtime on some of his last days in Neverland.

"I want to go home. I miss Father. I miss big, old, fluffy Lucy. I miss my toys and my bed. I want to go home, Wendy." His lower lip wobbled every time he finished, his big blue eyes glistening with unshed tears.

I normally hushed him, tucked him in, and left it at that. He and John were the ones that wanted to go on this adventure in the first place, who convinced me to go after Peter sprinkled us with pixie dust and taught us to fly. And every morning, he seemed to forget about our home in London as he gallivanted around the jungle with the Lost Boys, shaking his teddy to the beat of their drums.

But the night before it all happened, I didn't quiet Michael. I listened to all of his wants, hugged him to my chest while he blubbered, and I told him we'd be leaving in the morning; we'd go home as soon as we said our goodbyes and Peter could take us to the Second Star portal. As adventurous as this had been, I knew Father had to be worried sick about us—if Neverland time passed the same as London time, we'd been gone for nearly a week.

I calmed Michael down enough to tuck him into the bed he shared with John. The older boy was fast asleep with his face burrowed in a thick goose-feather pillow. I was just smoothing John's hair when I heard a faint noise behind me. Out of the corner of my eye, I saw a shadow flickering against the wall.

I turned, the skirt of my nightgown swishing around my legs, to find Peter stood in the doorway to the boys' room, his green eyes stricken. "But we're having so much fun," he pleaded. "You don't have to leave tomorrow. You don't ever have to go. Life here can be just as fun as in London."

The red of his hair caught the light from the lamp hanging on a hook next to the door, and his ripped pants still had stains on them from their romp in the mud earlier. I'd need to wash them and hang them up to dry before I went to bed myself, or they'd never be cleaned. Nothing had been cleaned until Peter had brought me here, it seemed.

I gave the boy a small smile and shook my head. "We have to leave tomorrow, Peter. Our visit has been lovely, but the boys need a normal life." I turned back at Michael's soft whimper to retrieve the teddy that had fallen on the hard-packed dirt floor, tucking it under the frayed quilt with him.

When I looked over my shoulder at Peter, something else flickered on his face. "I'll get you to stay, one way or another," he swore and stormed from the room.

I should have listened closely to his words. I should have believed in the threats veiled in his eyes. But he was just a boy of sixteen, a couple years younger than me, and I thought there was good in him, innocence.

The next dawn, some of the Lost Boys dragged me from my bed. They pushed me to and fro out of the treehouse I had learned to call home and laughed when I tripped or when dewy leaves smacked me in the face. Their behavior was peculiar and atrocious, even for wild boys, and when I told them as much with my voice hoarse from sleep, they only laughed again.

"Where are you taking me?" I snapped, lack of sleep making me cross. "Where are John and Michael?"

The boys grinned at me with a secret only they knew. Oliver, the oldest, leered straight down the neckline of my nightgown.

I fought a shiver at the look on his face, and I crossed my arms over my chest. "Peter wouldn't allow this." I tried not to let them see how fast my heart pounded against my ribs. "If he knew how you were treating his guest…"

"Peter told us to fetch you," was all I got in reply. They shoved and prodded me along until we reached the edge of the jungle.

I stumbled through the final barrier of tree branches and stepped into golden sun. I shielded my eyes with my hands, squinting against dawn's brilliance.

They'd led me to the Cliffs. I was certain the area had a proper name, but that's what Peter and the Lost Boys called them. The Cliffs were what Peter first showed us when he brought us to Neverland. If you stood at the very edge, where thick grass met rough-cut stone, you could see the ocean glittering all the way to the horizon. Captain Hook's pirate ship rocked in the waves, its white sails tied to the masts, no doubt holding dozens of scheming swashbucklers. Gorgeous mermaids swam in leisurely circles while the broad back of the infamous croc soaked up the morning sun.

I had asked Peter if the croc was the most dangerous sea dweller in Neverland. "No," he had said. "It's the mermaids. They long for flesh and blood. Whatever they don't eat, that's what the croc gets."

I should have listened closely to his words.

My name was called once, then twice, panic-edged. I stepped toward the voices, toward John and Michael, even though I couldn't quite see them. I scrubbed at my eyes, scrubbed at the alternating light and dark circles that blinded my vision.

When I opened them again, I could just make out the two smaller figures standing on the edge of the Cliffs. And a third figure, taller. Peter. John and Michael's hands were bound to their bodies with twine, Michael's teddy clenched in tiny fists.

"Peter," I said, dazed by the sun, by the shadows in his green eyes. Adrenaline pounded through my veins.

"Please don't make me do this, Wendy," he called, his voice still the picture of innocence. "You and John and Michael can all live happily in Neverland with us. If you don't, it'll just be ruined. Don't ruin my Neverland, Wendy. Stay."

I rubbed at my eyes again, heart thumping in my chest. "We can't stay, Peter. I'm sorry. The boys have school, and I'm sure our father is worried. You need to listen to me. What don't you want to do? Is this—is this one of your games?" I glanced from him to my brothers and back.

"I want to go home!" Michael burst out, but one sharp look from Peter quieted him. John grasped Michael's free hand in his own, his normally stoic expression exchanged for gritted teeth.

"You chose to come here," Peter retorted. "You like it here. You take care of us as a mother should, and we don't want you to leave. John and Michael can be part of the Lost Boys, and you can be our first Lost Girl. Endless fun, Wendy! No worries or fathers or school. Let the Second Star portal close and stay."

I wanted to tell him that if he wanted a mother, he should have stayed wherever he came from, just like all the Lost Boys should have. But the shadows in his green eyes gave me pause, as did the adrenaline that made my heart thud painfully against my ribs. "It can't be this way," I said finally, urging as much gentleness into my voice as I could. "I'm sorry, Peter. It's time for us to leave, please. This game needs to be over."

Peter clenched his jaw. "I'm not playing."

He pushed them.

I lurched forward, stumbled as my body tried to lock up in horror, and then my feet carried me to the edge of the Cliffs where I collapsed, staring down the white cliff-face, my hair rippling in the wind. My nails dug into the rocky edge as John and Michael screamed. They hit the water with two resounding splashes, John first, barely escaping being dashed to pieces on an outcropping of rocks.

Michael didn't know how to swim. But it didn't matter that he couldn't—my brothers wouldn't have time to think about escaping their ropes or sinking to the bottom of the sea. The mermaids were on top of them too fast.

Gorgeous blonde hair decorated with pearls and sea flowers, fins and tails colored silver and lavender. Their long nails and pointed teeth tore them to shreds, turned the aquamarine sea to blood.

John and Michael shrieked—for mercy, for Father, for me. Michael's teddy floated away from the carnage toward Hook's ship. And I could only watch, tears streaming down my cheeks, hands covering my ears, and jagged nails digging into my scalp as if that would help block out the sounds. My mouth hung open, but I couldn't tell if I was screaming or pleading with Peter over the noise.

Only when the shrieking and splashing stopped did I lower shaking hands from my ears. The sea still glinted red, but the mermaids chirped back and forth—the noise they made whenever they finished a good meal.

Blood rushed in my ears, making them ring. *Tha-thump.*

John wanted to be a lawyer. Little Michael just wanted to go home.

Someone touched my shoulder, then my chin, forcing me to turn my eyes away from the blood-soaked water. Peter's green eyes and thin, solemn face swam into focus. Ice ran through my veins.

Tha-thump. Tha-thump.

"Why?" I asked.

My voice rang hollow. My body felt hollow. For all it was worth, I could not dissolve into tears or start screaming at the boy. My ears rang as I tried to make sense of my brothers being here, alive and slinging mud at one another, one second, and torn limb from limb in the next.

Tha-thump. Tha-thump. Tha-thump.

Peter's face pinched, his nose crinkling as if he were the one in pain. "Because," he said like it was the simplest explanation in the world. "My Neverland is perfect with you in it, and you were going to leave because of them. I didn't have a choice, Wendy. Don't you see?" He grabbed my hands, his touch sending cold spasms through my skin. "You can stay now. It'll be alright. You have us."

The way he said my name—so innocent, so sincere—broke me. I jerked my hands from his grasp and clenched them in my lap. And though my voice refused to hold any of the grief that swelled in my chest, I stared into Peter's eyes to make sure he knew I meant every word. "You're a monster. I don't want any of *you*." My voice broke on the last word as I looked from Peter to the Lost Boys, at their mud-caked feet, skinned knees, their too-short trousers that I had washed and mended for them.

I'd cared for these boys.

Peter frowned and searched my face, searching for the lie in my words. But finding nothing but truth, he stood, shadows returning to dance in his eyes. "I didn't want to," he repeated, freckled nose wrinkled. "And I'm not a monster. I'll show you. You'll see why I had to do it."

He reached into the small pouch attached to his belt and sprinkled himself with gold dust from his pet fairy, Tinkerbell. Almost immediately, he began to float a few inches off the ground, the glitter twinkling on his skin in the sun. I remembered how enchanting the pixie dust had seemed back in London; how John and Michael begged to visit Neverland for just one night; how the dust tickled my nose and made me sneeze when Peter tossed it on me.

Tha-thump. Tha-thump. Tha-thump. Tha-thump.

Peter crossed his arms like a child over his bare chest. "Bring her back to the house," he commanded. "She'll see. We'll make her see."

My stomach curled into millions of knots at the devilish gleam on Oliver's face. The older Lost Boy scooped me up in his arms and groped my bottom. I let out a whimper, and Peter's frown deepened.

"*No*, Oliver. Be gentle with her. She's upset."

Oliver's back muscles stiffened, but he obeyed Peter's order without argument. Then Peter zipped over the treetops, back toward their treehouse home, leaving me alone with the boys.

I wanted to make Oliver let go of me as he walked into the forest, still slung over his shoulder. But the further we got away from the Cliffs, the more the ringing in my ears faded. The more the *tha-thump, tha-thump, tha-thump* of my heart slowed to finally accept the truth my brain already knew. John and Michael were dead. Peter was a monster.

And I was a prisoner of Neverland.

Back at the treehouse, Peter locked me in a room without any windows. Just wood on wood on wood, all yellowed with age. I stood by the door and listened to Peter tell one of the Lost Boys to guard me, and that he thought I was too upset to be around him right now.

I tuned out the conversation and sank down on the bed shoved into the corner of the tiny room, clutching a ragged patchwork quilt to my chest. Tears leaked from the corners of my eyes, and I didn't bother swiping them away. How could Peter do this? How could I have been so blind? I knew he didn't like the thought of us leaving, that it made him angry. But I hadn't thought anything of it, and that was the problem.

I hadn't thought at all. And now my brothers were dead because of me.

I stifled a sob and dropped the blanket to dig my fingers into my long, black hair. I had to get away from here, from Peter, and get back to London where I'd be safe. But how could I go back and live with myself, knowing my brothers should be by my side? Was there anywhere I could go to escape it all, or would the memories haunt me no matter where I ran?

Peter left me alone for the rest of the day, but he didn't stay gone long enough. After the lantern's light had flickered low, he unlocked the door to my room and entered, finding me lying on the bed. I had curled into a ball halfway through the day, fighting the agony coursing through me, fighting the sobs so the Lost Boys wouldn't hear me. But I immediately sat up and shrank away from him as he stepped into the room, the blanket twisting around my ankles. A flash of pain crossed his impish face as he watched me, then glanced at my two uneaten plates of food.

"Wendy," he said softly, "you need to eat."

"I don't want anything you give me," I snapped, but my voice was hoarse. "Get away from me."

Peter frowned and approached the bed, dirt-stained hands raised. "I know you're upset, but I need you to listen to me. You were going to leave us because of them. I had to kill them so you would stay." He sat down on the edge of the bed, and I cursed, scooting as far away from him as I could. "You're so caring, Wendy, and beautiful and smart. You make Neverland a better place, and my Neverland is perfect with you in it. I couldn't just let you leave."

He reached toward my face, and I shrieked, slapping his hand away and jumping to my feet, scurrying to the opposite side of the room. I clenched my hands into fists. "Don't *touch* me. You're a monster!"

Tears filled Peter's eyes, but I had no remorse, none for this demon boy in front of me. "I'll make you see," he whispered and left the room. The door latch thudded behind him. Only after he left did I release my clenched fists to reveal my shaking hands, bloody half-moon crescents in my palms from where I'd dug jagged nails into my skin.

Peter visited me every day for the next two weeks over mealtimes, pleading with me, trying to show me his side of the story. Trying to prove that he was innocent and good. But innocent people don't throw others off cliffs.

I failed my brothers. I couldn't ever change that. But the more time that passed and the more Peter spouted his lies, the angrier I got. Some integral part of me snapped, and I stopped being afraid of him. Instead, I spent my days and nights staring at the knotholes on the ceiling, burning with hatred. Memories of my brothers danced through my mind, of my favorite moments with them, moments I'd never get back—

John digging through old tomes, searching for clues about Jeremy Long's disappearance. I'd never seen him so passionate, so driven about anything before, and the memory made my heart crack. He would never bring justice to the world like he'd longed for.

And then there was Michael, splashing in the Lagoon without a care in the world. His teddy soaked through, the perfect picture of innocence.

Innocence that Peter had stolen.

I stared at the locked door of my room, fists clenched, my stomach full of knots. I couldn't change failing my brothers, but I could avenge them. I could tear Peter apart if I wanted to, if I had a way. And the next morning, when Peter visited my room and tried every lie he'd been spouting the past two weeks, I hissed, "Someday, somehow, I will rip you limb from limb until you know exactly how you've made me feel."

He stared at me, head cocked, those green eyes churning with anger, and I realized that he was not patient anymore. "You're staying," Peter spat after a moment's silence passed between us, both glaring at the other. "You're going to make Neverland perfect, even if I have to force you to see it." And before I could provide him with a proper retort, he grabbed my arm and tugged me out of the bedroom into the living area of the treehouse.

A cage set in the center of the room, its wooden door open wide, itchy straw scattered across its floor. My heart missed a beat. Peter had told me the cage was for things that didn't listen. I had assumed he meant animals or perhaps a strict punishment for a captured pirate.

Would I ever stop being so foolish?

Peter threw me into the cage, and I landed on my hands and knees. Straw pieces dug into my palms. By the time I scrambled to my feet and whipped around, he'd already slammed the cage door and locked it. We stared at each other through the bars, breathing heavily.

"You'll see," he hissed, nostrils flaring. That stupid phrase he repeated since he murdered John and Michael.

A fresh wave of anger washed over me, blurring my vision red. I spat at his feet. "I'll kill you before then."

Three weeks after being imprisoned, and a week of that spent in the cage, Peter and the Lost Boys decided to go for a jaunt to the Lagoon. Peter offered to take me, promising I could be free and have all the fun in the world if I chose to stay with him. I told him where he could stick his promises and then miserably hovered in my prison, dirty beyond belief, wondering how I was ever going to escape. I was stuck in a cage, and Tinkerbell the fairy was trapped in her glass jar in Peter's room, and Peter had taken my prison key with him.

They'd only been gone for a few minutes when I heard shuffling noises near the door. My heart sped up in my chest even as I willed myself to stay calm. They couldn't be back yet… or could they? What if Peter was back to taunt me? What if Oliver had managed to get the key away from Peter? Apprehension coiled in my stomach, and my mouth dried up.

I hated fear.

Eyes glued to the door, I watched the lock twist a little, click back into place, then turn fully. Before I could form a cohesive plan of protection in my head, the door flung open. In stepped a group of black-booted, heavy-footed men, led by none other than a pirate with a hook for a left hand.

All of the men stopped upon seeing me, and we stared at each other for a few seconds before Captain Hook cleared his throat. "Don't mind her. Start searching." His voice was gruff like waves beating against stone.

Hook's crew obeyed and hurried off into the separate rooms of the treehouse. Objects clattered, and drawers slammed throughout the house as the pirates began their search.

Hook walked up to my cage, observing me in silence, an almost frown on his face. I'd never seen the pirate captain before, but he was handsome with ebony skin, closely cropped dark hair, and smoldering brown eyes. I'd always imagined him to be aged with dirty, wrinkled clothes. Instead, he was only a couple years older than me, and his clothes were pristine—black pants, shiny leather boots, a cream white shirt that revealed part of his chest, and a swirling dark coat. His belt boasted a scabbard holding a gilded sword, as well as many smaller daggers and knives. Even his black hat was perfect, a red plume sticking straight out of it.

"You're from London," he said, drawing my gaze back to his face.

I stiffened. "How did you know that?"

Something akin to sympathy filled the pirate's eyes, and he shrugged. "The portal always takes Peter to London. I can only assume that's why you're here. And now I can tell from your accent."

I set my jaw and looked away, fidgeting with the hem of my nightgown. "What are you and your men looking for?"

"Tinkerbell," he replied. I met his eyes in surprise. "She's a friend of mine, and the other fairies say she hasn't been around lately. I could only assume Peter's been keeping her as a pet, and it's high time I set her free."

I swallowed at the horror of it. "She's in a glass jar," I mumbled. "Peter keeps her in his room. It's at the end of the hall."

Hook studied me for a few moments before nodding. "Arlo!" he called, and a pirate immediately hurried up to him. "She's in there. Get her, fast." He pointed at the hallway, and the crew member's boots echoed down the corridor.

Hook hesitated for a moment longer, glancing at the door, then down the hall, then at me before cursing under his breath. "You don't belong here. Come with me, and I can get you to safety."

I jerked my head up. "Why would you help me? You don't know me."

Hook's lips twitched, and a hint of sadness filled his eyes. "You're not the only one that's been kept in Neverland against their will." He stood up as Arlo reentered the room, brandishing the glass jar. The little fairy bounced up and down inside, banging her fists against the glass.

Hook took the jar, smiling at Tinkerbell, and she stopped slapping the glass when he spoke. "We're getting you out of here, Tink. Don't worry." The fairy blew him a kiss, and then he slipped the jar in one of his coat pockets and returned his gaze to me. "You have to trust me. I can get you out of here and back to London, where you belong. I'm the only shot you have."

Peter had rarely mentioned Hook. He had said they had a past and left it at that. It made me imagine all sorts of horrible things about the pirate. But Peter had lied and turned out to be the monster himself, so perhaps Hook was the better man. He was my only way out of this cage, my only way of getting revenge on Peter and going back to London. If Tinkerbell trusted the pirate, then perhaps I should too.

A chorus of singing, distant but still close enough to hear, filled my ears, and my blood ran cold. Hook stiffened as the sounds of Peter, and the Lost Boys whistled closer.

I nodded, scooting forward to grip the wooden bars. "Take me with you. Please."

The pirate captain provided me with a grim smile and wrenched the lock free from my cage with his hook. He opened the door. "Let's go," he hissed at his men.

I moved to stand, eager to be free and away from Peter, but my legs buckled beneath me. I gritted my teeth as spasms of pain shot through my body.

The singing grew louder.

"You can't walk?" Hook asked.

I fought through another wave of pain. "Not at the moment."

Hook bent down and scooped me up in his arms without another word. He kept the hook pointing away from me as best he could before nodding at his crew.

"Back to the beach."

The pirates descended the slope of the jungle, away from the boys' singing, the humidity drenching us all in sweat. Hook carried me the whole way, never once losing his footing or accidentally poking me with his hook. I wondered if he could feel how fast my heart was pounding, wondered if he sensed my worry that we might not make it to freedom before I was discovered missing.

The trees gave way to clear, glassy sand, and I squinted my eyes against the harsh sunlight glinting off the waves. My temples throbbed; my eyes were used to the dim light in the treehouse.

Hook swiftly walked over to a rowboat moored next to an outcropping of rocks and sat me down on one of the splintery benches. He sat next to me as his crew busied themselves with untying the boat and pushed it into the waves. Moments later, they hopped in and rowed us across the sparkling water.

I gripped the wooden bench, digging my nails into the rough wood. I'd never been on a boat before, not even back in London. I knew I would never get used to the rocking.

Hook watched me with intense brown eyes. "Relax. We're almost to my ship," he said. "You're safe now."

I said nothing, looking away to squint at the island of Neverland. I couldn't help myself as I scanned the horizon of trees and the rocky terrain of the volcano for Peter, strained to see if I could hear any noises other than the grunts of the men rowing and the splash of the oars in the water; the singing had long stopped. I stretched out my limbs as far as I could in the boat to get them working in case I'd need to dive into the water and swim for my life.

I would never be safe until Peter was *dealt* with.

The captain let me take a bath in his quarters while he attended to business on the main deck. I didn't know what I had expected the pirate's quarters to look like, but when Tinkerbell led me to the door and had me turn the knob, *clean* was not it.

Although small, the room was just as pristine as the captain's clothes. The cot in the corner was made just so, and the pillows were fluffed. His desk held neat stacks of papers and maps held down by copper paperweights. His coats and hats hung on rungs suspended over a two-drawer dresser, where I imagined he kept his other clothes. On top of the dresser was a wooden jewelry box. A hook suspended from the ceiling held an oil lantern just to the left of it. And just over the bed was a circular window with a black cloth pulled back to reveal the aquamarine ocean.

By the state of everything, he'd been here a long time.

Tinkerbell zipped to the jewelry box and unlatched the lid, startling me from my thoughts. On the underside of the lid was a small mirror, and in the box was an assortment of what looked like doll's clothes. The fairy laughed, a church-bell sound, and reached into the box, selecting a short green gown. I turned away as she dressed, heading over to the wooden tub in the corner of Hook's room. Water filled half of it, and a fresh bar of soap sat on a ledge notched into the wood. No steam rose from the water, but at least I would have a bath.

I undressed and sank into the tub. It was cold, freezing even, but the water felt good to my aching body. I lathered my hands with soap and began to wash. I scrubbed my body and hair three times before I felt decent again.

I stood to get out of the bath, and Tinkerbell flew over, handing me a towel. I stepped out, and water droplets pooled around my feet, little puddles on the wood. "Now I can figure out what to do with Peter. He needs to be dealt with. And Hook needs to explain how he's getting me back to London. Peter never told me how the portal works."

The fairy zoomed next to my right ear so her small voice could be heard. "Hook will help. All you have to do is ask." Then Tinkerbell flew toward Hook's dresser, waving at me with her hands and beckoning me to follow her.

Tinkerbell dove into one of the drawers and reappeared a second later, clutching a pair of trousers and a shirt from the bottom of the pile. They were old but clean and rather baggy. Fully dressed, I glanced down at my attire. The neckline on the shirt went lower than what would be appropriate in London, and the pants seemed to swallow my long legs. At least Father wasn't here to see me.

Tinkerbell flew up to my right ear. "Dinner will be served on deck. We should go up."

A sudden blush heated my cheeks and ears at the thought of being around Hook and his crew. My hair still hung loose and damp, and wearing Hook's clothes felt rather intimate. Would Hook say anything about the neckline of my shirt? But I had a plan to work on, revenge to seek. I couldn't think about how immodest my clothes might be.

Tinkerbell pulled a lock of my hair. "Come with me," she said in a sing-song tone. She fluttered to the closed door. I followed her out, the blush still burning my cheeks at the thought of showing off my new attire.

Tinkerbell led me to the main deck. I stumbled behind her, my limbs tense from being locked up, and the rocking ship didn't help. When we emerged into dying sunlight, the pirate crew sat around on deck, hovering close to an older man with graying hair dishing out stew from a large pot. All eyes focused on him, even as I approached, baggy clothes and all.

"Stay here," Tink said in my ear, and then the fairy flew into the throng. I obeyed, shifting from one foot to the other, wondering what to do, and feeling increasingly impatient.

Heavy footsteps approached. I looked up to Hook smiling at me with Tink perched on his shoulder. Heat rushed down my neck, but I stood my ground, waiting. The pirate captain stopped in front of me, his eyes traveling up and down my body.

"They fit," he said.

My whole body felt hot. "Mostly. Yes. Thank you." I didn't elaborate further, so Hook continued.

"Are you hungry? You look half-starved. Smee's made stew, and we have hardtack too. And ale. It's not quite fit for a lady, but . . ." Before he could finish, my stomach growled.

I pressed a hand to my belly, surprised at the wave of hunger and dizziness. Hook grabbed my arms, steadying me.

"Sit here." He lowered me onto a wooden crate, his tone filled with concern. "I'll go get you a plate. Tink, why don't you stay with her?" The fairy obliged, settling herself on my shoulder as Hook walked over to the gray-haired pirate.

"Did Peter not feed you?" Tink asked, patting my cheek.

My stomach growled a second time. "I ate just enough so he wouldn't force-feed me. I thought starving to death would be better than staying there."

Tinkerbell was silent for a few moments. "I'm glad Hook found us when he did. I'm glad he helped you escape."

"He offered an out," I agreed, watching as Hook wove his way through his crew with a tin bowl of stew in hand. "But I haven't escaped, not truly. Until Peter is dealt with, I won't be safe." I tried to finish quickly, but Hook was close enough to hear my final statement.

He frowned as he knelt down next to me, holding out the bowl of stew. "Peter won't find you, Wendy. Neverland is big. It will take him and his boys two days to search the island for you, and by then, we'll have taken you home to London. The portal closes at the end of the Second Star cycle in a couple of days, and if we take you there right as it closes, he won't have a chance to follow."

I took the stew, cupping the warm bowl with chilled fingers. "I want to go home, but not yet. Peter murdered my brothers. I want him dead." Anger flooded my stomach, and my heart pounded faster at my words. The bowl of stew shook slightly in my hands.

Hook's black eyebrows furrowed. "He killed your brothers?"

"He fed them to the mermaids," I mumbled, and I squeezed my eyes shut against the memories. "He thought they were the reason I wanted to leave Neverland, so he killed them to make me stay."

"Shit." Hook ran a hand through his short hair. "Stay here. I'll be right back." He left Tink hovering beside me and marched across the deck and down the stairs. Tink and I exchanged a frown, and a couple minutes passed before Hook reappeared, ducking his head so his hat wouldn't get knocked off. My heart stopped in my chest, and my ears rang at the item in his hands.

He stopped before me, holding a teddy bear out. Michael's teddy bear. "Then this must belong to you."

I dropped the bowl of stew, the liquid spilling out on the deck, and snatched the bear away from Hook, turning it over and over in my hands. Grief coiled my stomach into knots, followed by a rush of red-hot anger that warmed me from the inside out. The ringing in my ears ceased.

"I found it floating in the waves," Hook said. "I figured Peter must have brought more children back since the portal's open. I was hoping to return it to the Lagoon's shore in hopes whoever lost it could have it back."

I clenched the stuffed animal in my fists, unshed tears blurring my vision. The bear was missing one of the button eyes I'd recently resewn on. "I want him dead. I want him to pay for what he did."

Hook winced, squatting next to me. "Listen—"

"Wendy," Tink supplied.

"Wendy..." Hook repeated, voice gentle as if I were a scared child.

"I have to kill him!" I snapped, finally looking up from the bear to meet his gaze. "I want to go home, but he has to pay first. My brothers should be here with me, but he killed them!"

"I wouldn't even know how to catch Peter," Hook murmured. "We've avoided each other for so long. We'd have to think of a clever way to catch him and the Lost Boys, and by that point, the portal will be closed. It won't open again for three years, and by then, he will have found... Think of your home, of what I'm offering you."

My temper rose to a boil in my stomach. "Of course I want to go home! But first, I need to avenge my brothers, and I'll do it with or without your help. I'm not leaving without destroying him, until I take away everything that he's stolen from me. Do I make myself clear?" I drew my shoulders back, looked him square in the face, then gave the same look to Tink.

Tink looked at Hook. Hook looked at Tink. Tink flew up to say something in Hook's ear that I didn't catch.

Hook sighed and shook his head. "I'll go find you some ale and another bowl of stew."

"But—" I moved to stand, and Hook gently pushed me back on the crate. The side of my trousers caught on a loose nail.

"If I'm going to help you do this, you need your strength."

The Tale Continues in Volume Two

DISENCHANTMENT

Rachel Lawrence

I was only a girl
When he showed up
And threw his magic
Like stardust
Over everything

He promised me
Forever
His hand in mine
Only happy thoughts
As we flew high

I was too young
To know
That it's impossible
To never
Land
He dropped my hand

I felt so lost
Like a shadow
Of myself
A figment of
Some twisted imagination

So I built a hideout
For my heart
To keep out
Boys who refuse
To grow up

THE TINKER

Emily Barnett

FLIPPED THROUGH THE brittle pages of *Myths and Misconceptions* before slamming the dusty cover shut. The croc clock above my desk mocked me. *Tick. Tock. Tick.* Each second reminded me I was almost out of time.

"Wendy." The voice oozed around my ears, and I jolted, knocking over a serum which spilled and poofed my favorite pen into a purple cloud. Gritting my teeth, I turned to the crooked Sir Jim as he slunk into the workshop.

"What do you have for me today?" he drawled, his eyes like a storm.

I glanced at the bottle of fae dust. Its useless glow seemed to mock me. Ignoring it, I made my way to the wall of cordials, herbs, and whirring machines. My palms sweated. What could buy me an extension?

Sir Jim had given me one year to produce something impossible, and I was on day 345 with nothing to show for it.

Plucking a tiny airplane from a shelf, I shook it back and forth a few times and opened my hand. The plane zoomed around the room, its motor sputtering lavender fumes.

For a moment, Jim's eyes gleamed with greed.

The plane plummeted.

I grabbed at it, but it crashed into a pot of Jolly Jelly Jumpers, and the entirety of the jellies dashed about the room with violent exaltation.

Sir Jim cried out and swatted a blue bean out of his overly large nostril. Three beans became lost in my curls and yanked my scalp painfully.

"*Enough!*" Sir Jim screamed, his words laced with enough poison to kill an elephant. The Jolly Jelly Jumpers fell to the floor with sickening thuds. I rocked back on my heels.

Jim's eyes smoldered like embers in his ashy face. "Do you *not* want to save your brothers, Wendy, darling?"

I sucked in a breath, then wished I hadn't. The scent of rum and cigar smoke eagerly clung to his mustache and long, black hair. "I've done all you've asked." I tipped my chin up to meet his gaze even though my legs trembled. "I just need more time. I've almost—"

Sir Jim cackled with sardonic glee. "You're a Tinker. If you want more time, *tinker* a clock with more hours." He grinned. "But I still want what you owe me. Fuel to fly." He hooked a finger under my chin and pinched my flesh. His iron grip was like ice. "Tick. Tock," he whispered, then swept from the room like a wraith. I shivered in his wake.

My nerves were shot the rest of the day. The dust would either explode my machines, clog up the cogs, or do nothing at all. But it would *not* give me the fuel I needed.

Sir Jim had taken my brothers hostage when he learned of my Tinker magic. But he didn't comprehend that the process couldn't be forced, no matter how many times I told him. Not even Bell, my Tinker mentor when I was a child, had pushed her magic. I'd read her notes a hundred times, gleaning spells and mechanical insights, but still, I was only sixteen. After Bell was killed we hid my powers, and for all I knew, I was the only person left in London who had a touch of magic. Magic I wasn't sure even belonged to normal people like me.

But Sir Jim still found me.

Though it was legend Bell could turn dust to flight, she'd never written down the "how." I desperately needed the "how." After a year of trying to make a serum, a gadget, *anything* that had the semblance of weightlessness, I was stumped. Nothing worked. Perhaps my powers had been weakened by imprisonment, or I was paralyzed by the stress of what would happen to John and Michael if I didn't deliver. Lost forever at the hands of Jim Hooke—just like my beloved parents.

I was the only one who could save them. London's streets were lined with orphans, and no one cared if a few went missing.

The rest of the week was much the same. Disappointment. Tears. Tiny explosions.

Failure.

The last day of my captivity dawned with little hope. My brothers and I would either be released or killed once the clock struck midnight. And as the shadows grew longer and sunlight slipped into the heavy coat of night, my eyes stung with what would come. None of my dust spells had worked. Neither had my mechanics. Whimsical toys would get me nowhere.

Tick. Tock.

Only half an hour now stretched between life and death.

I paced the musty workshop, flinging old inventions from shelves as I passed and finding a small satisfaction in the oil that leaked from their parts, staining Sir Jim's floor like blood.

When the bell over the shop door announced a visitor, I spun. My blood was ice.

But it wasn't Sir Jim who came inside.

I blinked, forgetting to be afraid for a single, frigid breath.

A boy with hair as black as beetle wings stepped inside. He wasn't much older than me, and his eyes sparkled like a morning star about to blink out. The jacket he wore had an unnatural sheen, unlike the dull suits and top hats the men of London wore.

I hadn't seen another human besides Jim in an entire year.

The boy leaned against the shop counter, eyeing me. A silver watch peeked from his sleeve, but it didn't have an analog face. There were bright numbers on it, and I wondered, almost dreamily, if it didn't *tick* at all.

I cleared my throat. "Can—can I help you?"

Had he come to collect me, to do me in?

"I'm Peetur." The boy flashed me a smile, and my heart stalled for a moment. "I was rather hoping we could help each other, Wendy." His eyes roamed the shop and landed on a bottle of fae dust, shining gold like the sun.

"How do you know my name?" I asked.

Instead of answering, he sauntered over to the dust, uncorked it, and dropped a speck into his hand.

"Excuse me!" I hissed, no longer amused by his charms. I covered the ground between us in a single bound and snatched the bottle, corking it again. "What do you want?"

"To break you out of here."

I laughed darkly. "I can't leave." This boy was absolutely bonkers. Perhaps he'd gotten into Sir Jim's Tipsy Turvy Turkey brew when I wasn't looking.

Hooke would kill my brothers if I stepped foot from the workshop. And his men were always watching.

"Fae dust is wondrous on its own," Peetur said, gesturing to the bottle I gripped, as if he hadn't heard me at all. "It can cure illnesses or turn red hats to desk chairs. But to be able to *fly*, you need more than talent." He tapped the side of his head. "It's a state of mind."

I gritted my teeth. "My state of *mind* hasn't been so dandy since my brother's and I were taken prisoner, thank you very much."

"John and Michael?" He shrugged lightly. "They're good. My crew has them."

"Your... *what?*"

"Sorry it's taken me so long to find you. Our ship's been broken down on Earth for nearly a year, but I just caught word Jim had nabbed you." He raised a brow at me. "Ready to fly?"

"What? Where?"

Peetur shifted, and I noticed his eyes continued to gleam. Was this windswept boy made of starlight itself?

"My home planet, Everland." His gaze landed on the bottle in my hand. "You're the only Tinker left in this horrible world who can turn that dust into fuel. You're our way out."

"Another... planet?" I laughed derisively. "*Sure.* And I'm a mermaid's auntie."

He grew serious. "Are you?"

"Of course not!" I rubbed my eyes, glancing at the door. "You're *certain* you have my brothers?"

He raised one hand in a stoic gesture and covered his heart with the other. "I swear on the Second Star to the Right."

I wrinkled my nose. "Whatever *that* means." Tucking the bottle into my bag, I slung it over my shoulder. "Fine. Get me out of here, and I'll *try* to help you." Sir Jim would be back at midnight. We had minutes to vanish into London's shadows.

Peetur grinned as I hurried to the exit. But my hand stilled on the doorknob; my throat grew dry. "Jim's henchmen... they're right outside." I eyed the boy. He was tall but much too lanky for a fight with Sir Jim's men.

"I've taken care of them," he said with a wink.

My grip tightened, fingers whitening. If Peetur was wrong...

Something flickered in my stomach, and it felt like my magic pressing me to keep going. To trust. I sighed, glaring at him. I was taking a chance on this scoundrel. He'd better not let me down. But my alternative wasn't much better.

Taking a deep breath, I pulled open the door and stepped into the street.

It was empty.

The night air was close and dewy on my skin. And the sky... had it *always* felt so open? Tears leaked down my chin as I soaked in the sounds and colors and lights of a city I'd been kept from for far too long. It was overwhelming, yet still not enough.

My eye snagged on something hovering in the sky, and my jaw dropped.

A dark expanse blocked out a section of stars just above the building across from Jim's shop. The longer I stared, the more details I made out. It was round with tiny blinking lights and had a hard look as if it were made of metal. I wrinkled my brow and looked at Peetur. "Is that... your *ship*?"

He smiled proudly. "*Space*ship, actually. She's called the *White Bird*." Then he crooked a brow. "What? Were you expecting the *Mayflower*?"

"Uhm," was all I could manage.

A ship that cruised space in 1896 London? Other worlds?

I needed to sit down.

But Sir Jim wouldn't be far behind. "John and Michael?"

"Already on board."

I took a step forward, then glanced around the street nervously. "How have you kept the ship hidden?"

"It normally has a cloaking device, but I had to lower it to pick you up. That's why we came at night—slightly less conspicuous."

He held out his hand, palm up. An invitation. A chance. "Once we're in the air, we can take you wherever you'd like." His lips curved into a smile, but even so, there was a hint of shyness in his confident gaze. His pale cheeks flushed slightly. "Everland might be a nice change of scenery, though, Wendy." He said my name as if he knew me. As if he'd said my name a hundred times before.

"Have we met?" I asked. There *was* something familiar about him, even in the midst of the *un*familiar.

"I knew your parents before...." He swallowed thickly.

"Hooke," I spit the name like poison.

"Yeah, him."

"Wait—if you're from this Everland place, *how* did you know them?"

He hesitated. I blinked once, twice, three times before realization finally settled over me.

My lungs constricted. "Was Everland their home, too?"

"And *your* true home," he said with a sad smile. "Where do you think the Tinkers came from? You sure as rats don't have magic on earth."

"Everland." I tested the word on my tongue. The magic in my gut thrummed like a drum pounding out a song, and it was enough to stir me. To move me.

My eyes roamed over the London skyline. Big Ben inched closer to 12:00. Ten minutes before my deadline. If Peetur was right, this city was nothing to me, and the *White Bird* held everything I loved.

My stomach soured. "I've been trying for a year to make things fly for Sir Jim, and I... I can't."

Peetur's brow darkened, and my chest tightened.

I took a step back.

Had this been a mistake? I didn't know this boy—what *were* his true intentions? Had I traded one prison for another?

My breath turned shallow. My head spun.

"Whoa," Peetur said, taking my wrists in his hands. I tensed. "I'm not going to hurt you, Wendy. And I'm not going to force you to help me if you'd rather get your brothers and leave." His hands fell to his side. "I'll figure out another way." But there was little hope in this statement. I was the last Tinker that I knew of. There *was* no other way.

I straightened. "I'll try again," I said. "But what sort of state of mind do I need to be in to make something fly?" I asked, remembering what he'd told me in the workshop. "Because I have been devoted to finding a serum all year—"

"It will come." His smile returned.

Furrowing my brow, I glanced at Big Ben.

Tick. Tock. Tick.

Worry etched into me like ink in parchment. If I didn't find a way to make their ship run, we'd all be out of time. Who knew how many lackeys Hooke had crawling these streets like cockroaches.

Peetur stared at me with hopeful curiosity. His eyes like a wild storm—a storm I wasn't frightened of but drawn to.

Nodding once, I grasped his hand. He tugged me to a fire escape on the side of a building. As we climbed, my palms grew slick with nerves. This was impossible. I couldn't accomplish what he wanted.

But I *could* get Michael and John to safety.

Somehow.

Finally, we reached the top of the building, and Peetur flipped open his watch. I gaped as he spoke into it with a strange language, both lyrical and rough. After a moment, a rope ladder dropped from the ship's underbelly. And with it, a silhouette—a shadow, really—of a boy.

Peetur spoke to the shadow in the same melodic language, and the creature nodded as he held the ladder steady so we could ascend. I frowned at Peetur.

"Shade's harmless," Peetur said. "And great for sneaking into places. He's how I found you, actually."

"That's supposed to make me feel better?"

But the clock was still ticking. And this ladder led to my brothers.

Clenching my teeth, I climbed the slightly-swaying ladder. A London fog rolled in, but I held tight. *Almost there. Almost to them.*

When I reached the top, I swung my legs over the ship's edge. Peetur was right behind me, followed by Shade. I turned and was immediately accosted by children. All boys, at least twelve or under.

I frowned at the grease-smudged faces. "Where are the adults?"

"No adults here. The ship won't fly with them onboard," Peetur said and elbowed me lightly. "You barely made the cut-off."

But I hardly felt his jab. Hardly registered his words.

The crowd parted, and the two boys I had given everything for ran toward me. They looked older, and John had a bruise on his right cheek, but they were *here*. Smiling. In one piece.

We collided, and a laugh tore from my chest. They smelled like dirt and youth and ... and *home*. A relieved sob broke through me, and I clung to my brothers with such fervor Michael let out a squeak.

"We're okay, Wendy," he sniffled into my shoulder.

His little voice sent me spiraling back. Back to a world where I wasn't a prisoner. Where I was free to run, to climb trees, to laugh and dance. To Tinker new creations—part machine and part magic.

Pangs of memories swirled through me.

Laughter skittering down the hall. Cherry pies on Sundays. Stick sword fights. Playing pirates at the creek. Our parents reading bedtime stories about worlds where magic existed. Quilt forts. Star-gazing.

Childhood.

Warmth flooded my chest and down my arms. My whole body warmed as if I were sitting too close to the hearth. My brothers stepped away, staring at me in confusion. But Peetur strolled forward and opened my bag, then plopped the bottle of dust in my hands. *"What are you—?"* I began.

The dust changed from gold into a blinding white. My pulse quickened.

"That's it, Wendy," Peetur said. "The right state of mind."

"What is it?" Michael whispered, his glasses fogging.

"Our ticket out of here," a round boy said.

The warmth seeped out of me, save for my fingers that gripped the bottle.

Peetur nodded to the round boy. "Tootles will take the fuel now if that's alright."

"Right." I handed the bottle to the boy. "Of course."

"Alright, crew. Positions!" Peetur shouted, and the children scattered. "Wendy?" he asked, turning to me and my brothers. "Where would you like to go?"

John and Michael were looking at me expectantly. Blankly.

Our parents were dead. We had no other family. And if we stayed in London, we'd only be hunted. I ruffled John's hair and looked at Peetur.

"Our true home."

While the crew got into place, I drifted to the front of the ship filled with blinking lights and knobs and tubes and wires I couldn't even begin to understand. I stopped at the large glass windows. The vast stars winked over the city.

Could we truly be free?

I could just make out Big Ben from the corner of the window.

Tick, tock. 12:00. *Bong. Bong. Bong...*

Out of time.

Peetur stood behind an out-of-place vintage boat wheel in the center of a panel, like it *had* actually been taken from the *Mayflower.* John and Michael were already strapped into seats behind him.

After a tense moment, Peetur pressed a button. "Get that fuel loaded yet, Tootles? You know he'll be unhappy I've stolen from him again."

I narrowed my eyes. "*Again?* Do you know Sir Jim?"

The crew's quiet laughter rustled around us like dried leaves. But Peetur didn't laugh. His eyes took on a dangerous hue. A storm I wasn't sure I trusted anymore. A spark of dark familiarity. Almost like—

"Oh, I know him," he growled. "Bloke's my father." His gaze shifted to mine. "I'm his long-lost son, and I bloody hope to stay that way."

My throat turned to sand.

His eyes. Wild and stormy. Just like Sir Jim's.

My stomach dropped, and I steadied myself on the cold wall beside me. Peetur left his station and touched my arm. "I should have told you, I know. But I needed you to trust me."

I wrenched my arm away. "*Don't touch me,*" I spat. My eyes hardened even as Peetur's softened. "How can I trust someone who keeps things from me... and... the son of that *monster?*"

I wasn't running from my troubles; I was stepping on board to a whole lot more of them. And I was bringing my brothers along for the ride. Nausea rose in my throat, and I swallowed hard.

"It's a trust I'd like to earn back one day, but for now, we need to go." He looked back at his station. "Come on, Tootles!"

Earn *back?*

My eyes swept his face, trying to recall if we'd met before. There was something familiar about Peetur but not enough to dredge up memories. And besides, it wasn't the time. Actually, we *had* no time.

"Won't Jim chase us *because* you're his son?" The bait had only grown more enticing for him: a Tinker *and* his child. Perfect.

"Don't worry, Wendy," Peetur said. "I've fought the man for years. Hooke has forgotten what it's like to be a kid—to dream and to wonder. It will take him a long time to figure out a way back home." He smiled.

Home.

Everland. A planet as mysterious as the boy who held galaxies in his gaze. Who somehow held my past in his memories.

The ship rumbled under my feet, and I swayed, grabbing a seat. The crew whooped in jubilance, and my anxiety lessened as Peetur ran back to his wheel, then pressed a lever down. The ship soared over Big Ben and into the deep heavens.

Tick. Tock. Tick.

Though worry still lingered, and trust wouldn't come easy, I couldn't help but grin in relief. I'd found my brothers. They were alive, and I'd make sure they stayed that way.

Sir Jim thought I'd run out of time, but with a little help from his rogue son, I'd figured out a way to tinker the clock.

The Tale Continues in Volume Two

LITTLE BOYS DON'T GROW UP

Anne J. Hill

I sit, reading the words I once wrote about you
And I'm realizing they are no longer true
And I have no idea what to do
Other than to find somebody new

I try to remember who you used to be
Or at least who you were around me
But him I can no longer see
Is this how things were meant to be

I can't find the man I used to adore
Somewhere locked behind all those doors
Maybe my judgment was just poor
When I let you shove me onto the floor

And there I acted as your doormat
And I let you hit me with your bat
Until I lay on the floor flat
You wore my crown like a toy hat

Don't make promises you don't plan on keeping
Don't use words that have no meaning
Stop saying I'm overacting
Cuz I trusted you to not be play acting

All I wanted was an apology
Or do you not see all you've done to me
I'm tired of being the one you leave
I can't keep trusting the stories you weave

Am I really the one to blame
For counting on you to bear your own name
Or is that just too tame
For someone who carries all of your 'shame'

I don't know what else I expected
You'd sit there, making me feel infected
Cuz I didn't fit your mold, so you injected
Your standards in me then called me rejected

I should have seen this coming
Little boys have a way of not growing
And I've just given up caring
When you act like life is despairing

I'm tired of waiting here
For you to suddenly appear
I'm no longer captive to this fear
That you will never again be near

THE ISLAND OF FORGOTTEN THINGS

Cassandra Hamm

ERHAPS TODAY IS the day I'll drown.

Sunlight paints the ocean in flashes of white as I swim away from Neverland. Arms burning, I slice through the water, stroke after stroke after stroke. Though my lungs ache, I refuse to stop. *There has to be a border somewhere. I just haven't found it yet.*

Or maybe there is no escaping Neverland.

I heave my head out of the water and suck in precious air. The sun beats down on my skin, warm and balmy. Faint, feminine laughter drifts from the shallows—amusement at something Pan said? Adoration for their fearless leader?

No one noticed you leave. They wouldn't care if you never came back. Certainly not Pan. She'd probably rejoice.

Water covers my ears and garbles the chattering of the other girls as I sink below the surface, arms outstretched, legs limp. Watery echoes fill my ears, soothing, gentle, a welcome reprieve from Pan's tantrums.

My eyes slide open. Dozens of shades of blue twine together in a sensuous dance—*no, not sensuous, anything but that*—and I turn my attention to the fish inhabiting the lagoon. Blood red and sun-ray yellow and black as my sins.

Several feet beneath me, a jagged crack runs along the ocean floor, splitting the coral. Empty ocean surrounds the crevasse as though the fish fear it.

I surface, taking deep lungfuls of air before plunging deeper, deeper. Carefully, I reach inside the crack.

No tingling sense of magic. No portal leading to the world I came from. Just mud and stone and bits of broken coral.

I stare at the useless crack until my eyes burn and my mouth wants to scream, and my lungs constrict, squeezing tighter and tighter like hands around my neck—

hands and breaths and oh God make it stop

Something wraps around my arm and yanks me upward. I thrash.

let go of me, I don't want this, I don't

My head breaks through the surface. I heave in desperate breaths and gaze at a dark-skinned girl.

Not him. Just Ro.

Ro's lips curl downward. Dozens of dripping black braids frame her angular face. "You were gone too long, Gen," she says, releasing my hand.

"I'm fine." An immediate reflex.

The gentle pressure of her dark eyes makes me want to confess my every sin—but she already knows them.

"I was testing it." I gesture to the crack. "Seeing if it was a way out. Should've known better."

Ro sighs. "Gen…"

"Pan's not all powerful. There has to be a way out." I've swam every inch of the lagoon and explored as far as I dared into the ocean beyond—as far as Ro has allowed. Without her, I would've swam until my body gave out and my destiny was the bottom of a forgotten sea.

I'm not sure I've forgiven her for stopping me.

"What if there isn't?" Ro speaks softly, like I am glass ready to break. "What if you could never leave?"

The words slam into my skull and rattle through my brain. *Never leave, never leave, never leave.* "I can't," I choke out. "I can't laugh and smile and pretend like... like I'm not ..."

hollow like his eyes as they burned into mine

"I know." Ro touches my shoulder. Even though I see her reach for me, I still jump.

I drop my gaze to the ripples. *Breathe, Gen. Breathe.*

"How do you do it?" I whisper. "Don't you *want* to leave?"

Her jaw clenches. "I don't want to go back to that."

I remember the day Pan brought Ro to Neverland. Though saltwater eased the burns that marred Ro's deep brown skin that day, the scars remain, jagged and deliberate, in the shape of cigarette butts. Does she remember her past, or does it flit through her mind like wisps she can't quite grasp or nightmares that fade upon her waking?

hands like hooks and lips like brands

My chest tightens, lungs squeezing, squeezing, squeezing, and I shrink into my skin. *Disappear. No one would care.*

"Gen." Ro's gentle voice.

I cling to it like an anchor, holding me above the water. I will not let myself drown. Not today, at least.

I throw myself back into the rhythm of swimming and focus on the strokes—*left, right, left, right*—instead of the emptiness inside. The water shifts from indigo to cerulean to turquoise. I pause at the lagoon's edge. Neverland stretches before me—sugar-pale sand, palm trees stretching into a cloudless sky with leaves like grabbing, grasping hands.

please let go of me, please, please, please

I swim farther into the lagoon and watch the other Lost Girls. Liss and Ky splash each other with high-pitched squeals. Hel floats on her back and soaks in the sun's rays, and Nic tackles Ari. They sink below the surface.

My breath catches—*what if they don't come back up?*—but they emerge, dripping and sputtering. A shadow passes over Ari's face, there an instant, gone the next. Did Nic forget that Ari needs a warning before she's touched?

Pan bursts from the water like a resurrected goddess. Her sodden, close-shorn hair, normally a vivid orange, paints a blood-like stain against her scalp. She laughs, eyes crinkled, teeth flashing.

Liss and Ky stop their splashing to watch. Hel, Nic, and Ari paddle toward Pan, drawn by some invisible force, as though she is the sun and they exist for her. And maybe we do. Maybe we all exist for her.

Pan's eyes meet mine, flicking from me to Ro. I'm sure she realized that we strayed from the lagoon but chose not to say anything—yet. She'd be even more furious if she realized exactly how far I swam today. Part of me wants to tell her what I did just to watch her seethe.

"Swim time is over," she announces. "Now we're going to explore."

Two of the only things we do on this forsaken island. Eat, sleep, swim, explore—like there's anything else to explore at this point—play games, and pretend, always pretend. Pan's little paradise.

With a sigh, Ro starts toward the beach along with the others. Part of me wants to stay right here in the water—or maybe to sink down, down, down and never come back up. Instead, I swim slowly, leisurely. That'll annoy Pan—her orders not being followed absolutely.

Sure enough, when I drag myself onto the sand and stand lazily to attention, Pan's eyes are hard and flat, like a gold coin. Sunlight gleams off the thimble hanging around her neck. "We're exploring now," she says.

"You said we were swimming today," I say. "That's what you decided. A day at the lagoon."

Pan's mouth tightens into a thin line. The breeze sharpens, tugging at our wet clothes. "Okay, yeah, but I changed my mind!"

Like she always does. Like she has for the past... who knows how many years.

How long have I been trapped here? A thought that won't go away.

I shake my head to dispel the flashes of memory—images, pieces I don't want to connect. Or maybe I do. *Who was I?* The damp sand is a balm against my bare feet.

"I like swimming." Ky wraps her arms around her forever-flat chest and shivers. "I wanna keep swimming, Pan."

"Well, I don't," Pan says.

"And your word is law," I mutter.

Pan's nostrils flare. "You wanna say something, Gen?"

The Lost Girls watch with wide eyes. Would any of them support me if I challenged her? Ro, maybe, but she loves this place too much to leave it.

God only knows why.

Let it go, a voice inside me whispers. *Let Pan play her games and run her island.*

Ages and ages ago, Pan climbed through my bedroom window. Moonlight streamed against her back and turned her face to shadow as she held out a freckled hand.

"You wanna get out?" she asked with a dazzling smile.

The longing to escape was so desperate it seared my bones. I remember wondering if she would hurt me too before nodding and taking her hand. *Anything would be better than this,* I thought.

"You'll never have to see him again, I swear," she said. "You're safe now."

Then I was flying, compressed into tiny bits, surrounded by pinprick-sharp lights, unable to breathe, until we found Neverland.

It is everything and nothing, beauty and numbness. It is dazzling and electrifying and mind-numbing. It is inescapable.

"We could split up," Ro says. "Some could play in the water; some could explore. You could lead the explorers, Pan, and someone else could lead the swimming party."

"Someone like *you?*" Pan's words crack like hands against flesh.

She and Ro were both thirteen when the magic stopped their aging, but even though Pan's been here for God knows how many years, Ro seems older. Grown up—a forbidden concept in Neverland.

"You wanna be leader? Is that it, Ro?"

"That's not what I'm saying, Pan."

Pan's voice pitches high. "Liar!"

The sand shivers beneath me. I don't know if it's my imagination or if it's something more—if Pan somehow has a hold on this island so that it does her bidding. One more way to control us.

"No," Ro says, "I just thought maybe—"

"Liar, liar, *liar!*" Pan stomps her foot. *"I* saved you. *I* brought you to Neverland. To *my* secret, special place. And you want to take it away from me!"

"Would it kill you to listen to someone else for once?" I say. "It's always about *you,* Pan. What *you* want. What about what *we* want?"

Pan's shoulders snap back so violently I jump. The air thickens with the promise of a storm as the sky softens from bright blue to muted gray.

You'll stop now if you know what's good for you, her eyes say. But I'm done bowing.

"What do *you* want, Liss?" I kneel before the perpetual four-year-old. Her hair hangs in wet strands around her face, and her eyes fill with sudden tears. "Go on," I say. "*I* wanna know, unlike Pan."

"I—I—" She darts a glance at Pan, then blurts, "I wanna go *home*, Gen. I miss my da."

"Your da?" Pan swells up, all five feet of her. "The one who beat you 'til you couldn't breathe? *That* da?"

"Sorry," Liss mumbles, hands shaking. "Sorry, sorry." She keeps repeating it as though her life depends on it. The blankness in her sea-blue eyes tells me she sees someone else instead of Pan.

Pan pats Liss's head. Liss jumps, her eyes focusing again before they blur with tears.

"It's okay," Pan says. "I know you are. Hey, no crying, remember? This is a happy place."

Liss bites her lip hard, as though that will stop the wetness coursing down her chubby cheeks. Her head bobs up and down.

"Good," Pan says.

Something boils inside me, hot and fierce. She always does this— throws fits and twists our words until we say *sorry, sorry, sorry,* like we haven't spent our whole damn lives apologizing and bending over backward. *She said we'd be safe here.*

"This isn't right, Pan," I say. "You know it's not."

Pan turns to face me. Her eyes are over-bright. "You don't know what you're talking about, Gen."

"We shouldn't be here. None of us."

"Neverland is *perfect.*" Her words come out shrill. "You should be *thanking* me. I saved you, remember?"

"Yes, you remind us all the time!"

Lightning crackles in the air. "Because it's *true!* If you would just listen to me—"

"I'm done listening to you!"

A sharp, shocked breath from the girls. Pan's mouth opens, then shuts.

"People always forced us to do this, do that, stay quiet or else," I say. "It's not supposed to be that way here. This is supposed to be a safe place."

"It *is* a safe place."

"Open your eyes, Pan." I throw my hands up, gesturing to our sanctuary, our fortress, our prison. "We try to forget. But forgetting isn't healing."

She freezes.

I've tried to push it away—we all have. We laugh and smile and pretend, but it's still there in the back of our minds—the reason Pan brought us here. She might try to smother it with magic. She might lull us with sweet coconut milk and carefree days in the sun, but *we know.*

We are violated. We are broken.

"He's *there.* In the back of my head. Haunting my every move, and I just—" My throat tightens, cutting off the words.

In my dreams, a man with a hook reaches into places he shouldn't. His breath is warm and sickly-sweet against my neck as he murmurs, "It'll all be over soon." His smile is as white as sun-bleached bones.

please stop, please, please, please

But my words vanish into the air as though they never existed. As though *I* never existed.

He is from my life before. I know it like I know this island back to front. *He's waiting for me.* The thought chokes me as effectively as he once did.

"I remember, too." Ro tucks her braids behind her ear in what I recognize as a self-conscious gesture.

"Me too." Hel wrings her thin, scarred hands.

The other girls murmur agreement. Liss' eyes shimmer. In them is more pain than any four-year-old should have endured.

Pan stares at us, her face slack. She seems almost lost.

"I did this... for *you,*" she whispers. "All of it. What I gave up... "

"What did you give up, Pan?" Ari looks smaller than ever, a ten-year-old trapped in a never-aging body.

Pan is quiet for a long moment. "I couldn't stand it any longer. I wanted somewhere far, far away where he—where he could never hurt me again. So I begged the faeries for a safe haven. They agreed to create Neverland—for a price. My freedom."

I clench my jaw. *She doesn't deserve your pity or your thoughts or your tears.*

"Now I'm tied to this island." Pan lowers her gaze to the sand. "I can't leave it."

There is a heavy silence, broken only by the whistling of the breeze through the palm leaves. I focus on the warmth of the sand beneath my feet.

"Can you give control of the island to someone else?" Ro asks.

"I don't know. Maybe." Pan fingers the thimble nestled in the hollow of her throat. "This is what the faeries gave me. It's bonded to an acorn charm that lies deep within the island. They feed off each other. My happiness, my peace, they make the island beautiful. If I'm upset... "

I think of the cracks in the ocean floor. Of the times I found the food decaying and the flowers shriveling. Of the tropical storms that howl in when Pan's rage burns white-hot.

She hasn't just found a way to control the island. She *is* the island. She is the reason I'm miserable. *She is the problem.*

Her hand tightens around the thimble. "And I'm not going to give it to *you,* if that's what you're asking," she adds snippily.

"I don't want that," Ro says. "I just wanted to see if I could help you. I'm sorry you're dealing with this."

I'm not. I'm furious. How *dare* Pan assume what we want. How *dare* she make us play to her whims. No wonder we've never been allowed to upset her or disappoint her. She can't have her perfect little paradise crumbling. That would mean she'd failed.

Pan's golden eyes flick to me, her first Lost Girl. "I wanted to save other people from what I went through. So I rescued you. I didn't think... I mean, Gen, I thought you'd be happy."

Happy.

The word echoes through my head like a command. *Stay happy. Don't think about roving hands or wayward mouths. Don't bother anyone with your pain. Be* happy, *damn it!*

She *knows* what I came from. I was sixteen when she found me— older than any of the other girls, old enough to remember every moment in excruciating, vivid detail. *Forget,* she told me. *Move on.*

I am an explosion waiting to happen. I am a storm ready to break. I am lost.

Don't you dare tell me to be happy.

Pan turns away and stomps toward the jungle before I can unleash my fury. Smart girl. "We're going exploring, and you're not invited, Gen. Or you, Ro."

"You're doing it again, Pan!" I cry.

She doesn't even flinch.

Hel's face is creased in a frown. The girls aren't used to anyone questioning Pan. But it's about time someone did. Screw the island.

"Oh, yes, run away like the spoiled little bitch you are!" I scream after her.

Pan halts just before the treeline. Tension screams from the line of her squared shoulders, her stiff limbs. Thunder rumbles too close.

"God, I'm so sick of it! The way you ignore us when we do or say something you don't like, as if ignoring it will make it not right. As if our opinions don't matter. As if *we* don't matter. It was supposed to be *different* here, Pan!"

"Gen, wait—" Ro says.

"I'm getting the hell off this island, and I'm taking them with me." I fling my arm toward the stunned Lost Girls. "Then it'll just be you and your precious Neverland. Throw all the damn tantrums you want. Just keep me out of your issues."

Pan whirls around. A storm crackles in her eyes. "You don't have to tell me how broken I am. I *live* with it."

A jagged fissure splits the sand. The girls scream. I stumble backward.

Pan stalks toward us like a predator who's caught a scent. She lifts her tunic enough for us to see her tanned abdomen. Thick, red lines criss-cross her stomach.

"That's not even the worst of it. It's what he did up *here.*" She taps her head.

The sand blackens beneath us. Palm trees tremble and split, their leaves shriveling. The sickly-sweet scent of decay fills the humid air. Sin-dark clouds gather on the horizon and race toward us with unnatural speed as the ocean roils and churns.

"I try to keep it away, but it builds and builds, and I just *can't—*"

Ro lunges toward Liss just as a palm tree cracks in half, plunging toward where the little girl was. They roll on the darkening sand, Liss wailing.

Nic and Ari flee toward the water as more trees crash against the ground. I stare, open-mouthed. Pan holds her head and tears at her red-gold hair. The heavens dump fat raindrops that sting and slap like merciless hands.

I did this. I pushed her too far.

The ground continues to split, exposing sizzling, smoking magma. Hel screams. Her legs pinwheel as she tries to outrun the crumbling earth.

I shake myself from my stupor and sprint toward her. Our hands find each other, slick with sweat and rain, and I drag her like I'm running from the hook-handed man, and he is gaining, and I just need somewhere safe, *please, please, please*—

"Gen!" Hel tugs me to a stop, nearly yanking my arm from its socket.

I blink hard through the rain, trying to gather my spinning thoughts. The crack halts a few meters away. Did Pan do that? Does she still have some control over the island?

Does she actually still care about us?

The wind pulls my hair free of its braid and whips it around my face. Rain lashes at my skin. The Lost Girls scream and flee from this paradise-turned-nightmare, but there is no leaving Neverland. I know. I've tried.

Lightning cracks the sky, reflecting off the thimble. The source of the faeries' magic. The heart and soul of Neverland.

Pan doesn't notice my presence until I lunge for her, grasping for the thimble. She thrashes, slapping at my hands.

Take the thimble and it will end—

"Let go of me!" she screams.

An image fills my mind—the man who haunts my dreams, arms tight around me, body pressed against mine. "Let go of me," I try to say, but his hand covers my mouth.

"Shh," he says. "Don't pretend you don't want this."

I beg and scream until my throat is raw, until I am used and spent and *hollow, hollow, hollow*

In the present, I let go of Pan and collapse against the sand. "Okay," I say, barely audible above the storm. Rain pounds against my back, as though punishing me for trying to take away her world, her choice. *I won't be like him. I'll never be like him.*

Pan slowly lifts her face. Her unshuttered eyes pierce right to my core.

The wind eases, just enough for me to notice. The rain feels more like a massage than a beating.

"I just wanted you to be happy," she whispers. "All of you. People like us, we have to grow up too fast. I wanted you to have a real childhood. You know that, right?"

"I know." Tears fill my eyes and mix with the raindrops. "But then you forgot."

Heavy sobs wrack Pan's tiny frame.

The other girls gape at her as though unsure how to proceed. "It's okay, Pan," Ari says in an unsure tone.

"No," I say. "It's *not* okay. What she went through, what *we* went through, it will never be *okay.*"

Ro nods. I wonder about the cigarette burns, if she wakes up from nightmares like I do.

Pan presses a hand to her mouth. "I can't do this. I thought I could, but I can't. It's too much. I'm…"

"I know," I say.

I stare at the tiny thimble hanging around her neck. The burden she's been carrying for who knows how many years. The burden I almost stole from her just to make the pain stop. But I'm just as bad as Pan. My demons would've destroyed Neverland once and for all.

Ro stretches out her slender brown hand. I note the puckered skin on her palms. "Give me the thimble, Pan."

"But . . ." Pan hugs her knees to her chest and rocks back and forth, back and forth. "I can't just let Neverland fall. This island, it's all we have."

"It won't fall." Ro meets Pan's gaze. "I'll take care of it. I promise."

Pan's lips tremble. "You know how I feel about promises."

promises are made to be obliterated into a thousand pieces like glittering, vengeful stars

"I know," Ro says.

We hold our breath. Pan shakes, eyes squeezed shut, arms wrapped around her knees. She looks small and thin, like she could blow away.

I barely stop myself from reaching for her. She doesn't deserve my comfort. But maybe I want to give it anyway.

"You don't have to be Neverland if you don't want to be," I say quietly. "You can let go."

Pan's shimmering eyes meet mine. Then, she unlatches the chain. The thimble glimmers, small and silver, as she holds the necklace out to Ro.

A faint smile touches Ro's lips as she accepts it. When she places it around her neck, the world stills—the waves settle to soft lapping, the sky brightens to baby blue, and the wind gentles to a tender ocean breeze. Fallen trees still litter the ground, but the sand returns to a healthy golden brown, and the fissure thins.

Ari grabs Nic's arm and squeezes tightly. Hel hugs her arms to her chest, looking either like she's about to laugh or cry. Ky presses her hands to her mouth, and Liss just stares, looking lost. Like the Lost Girl she is.

Maybe we don't have to be lost anymore. Maybe we can find each other.

Ro closes her eyes. "I feel the barrier. It won't be too difficult to open."

An escape. My breath catches. Could it finally be... ?

"You can stay if you want to. We'll have lots of fun together, but we'll heal, too. And if you want to leave ..." Ro looks right at me.

I blink back sudden tears. I knew it would come to this, and yet... What will I do without Ro's calm, steadying presence? Her pulling me back from the edge?

She'll always be a thought away, a voice inside my head, reminding me what I need. No matter where I go, I can't get away from my Ro.

"I know you have to go, Gen." Ro smiles, just a slight turn of her lips. "Go face your demons."

I swallow hard and give her a single nod. Then I sweep my gaze over the girls. "Anyone else? Hel? Liss?"

They look at me, then at the ocean, then at each other.

"Not yet," Hel says, just a whisper. "But eventually."

I nod at her, wondering how old I'll be by the time she leaves this never-aging island. Will she even recognize me?

"I wanna swim," Liss says. "I don't wanna get hurt."

I bite my lip so hard I taste blood. "But your da, Liss. I thought you wanted to see him."

"She wants to stay, Gen." Ro holds my gaze. "Let her choose that."

It stings, but I nod. My heart feels heavy. Will I be on my own again, facing the hook-handed man? *Should I stay?*

But I can't. My spirit strains against these borders. I need to *fly* and *feel* and *live* again.

I hug the girls one by one, holding extra tight to Liss. My sisters. Pieces of my heart I will never regain.

"Will you ever come back?" Hel says.

I know the answer, but I can't bear to see her face crumple. So I say, "I don't know. Maybe."

"Liar." Pan's voice is barely a croak.

I turn to her with surprise. Her eyes are red-rimmed, her nose and lips swollen, but she manages a sad smile.

We were like sisters once. Maybe we could be that way again.

"Come with me," I say. "It's not your island anymore. You can go wherever you want, be whoever you want. We could . . ." The words catch, but I force them out. "Um, we could do it together. Heal, I mean. Really heal. We Lost Girls have to stick together, you know."

Pan doesn't answer. I wish I could take the words back. It's stupid to think that our past could be so easily forgotten, that things could return to the way they were—or *better* than they were. "Never mind," I mumble.

Pan crashes against me, holding me tight, her head pressed against my shoulder blade. I gasp at the suddenness, at the rightness. Maybe it isn't so stupid to think that we could be close as sisters again. Not yet, but someday.

"Thank you," she says. "Genevieve."

The name crashes against my consciousness and triggers an onslaught of memories, long buried thanks to Neverland's magic. *House and friends and sky and brother and good and and and*

There is more than the hook-handed man. There is *life*.

I lean against Pan, full and empty all at once, and gaze at the shores that I—that *Gen* once inhabited. *Goodbye, Neverland. Goodbye, Gen.*

A round, glowing hole opens a few feet away. In it, I can see glimpses of buildings and steel and *people*. So many faces, so many untold stories. So many memories waiting to be made.

"I'm scared," Pan says.

"I know." I take her hand and lead her toward the portal. I am exploding with light and warmth and color. I am ready. I am Genevieve. "Time for us to grow up."

THE LOST CALL IT HOME

Kayla E. Green

I'm trapped in the labyrinth of my mind
Self-deprecating whimsies, I continuously find.
Though the end to the maze eludes me
The reflective glass causes me to see
Myself and I mourn for her…
Regret stands before me at every turn of the corner
Tears fall incessantly
For the girl I once was, and for the woman I never shall be.
How did I arrive here?
With a heart so full of anxious thoughts and fear.
Why can't I escape the lies of Peter Pan?
Why'd I let myself get brought into Neverland?
There's a reason why the lost call it home.

THE BOY CALLED REAPER

Julia Skinner

WOULD YOU LIKE *me to tell you the story of the invisible boy?* Once upon a time, there was a boy no one could see unless they were dying. And in Haven Fair, no one died unless they wanted to, or… unless the boy came for them, and he only ever came for children.

I know, I know. It's a strange thing, isn't it, little one? To think of a world where death is not so prominent. But such a place does exist. I was born there, after all.

Legend claimed that he was an orphan, abandoned by his mother, with only the wind left to watch over him. She taught him to fly and showed him the secrets hidden in the depth of space. The boy was known throughout the realm by many names. Some called him a ghost, some Pan; the people of Haven Fair came to call him the Reaper, for he came every second year, on the first day of fall, to steal a life.

Now, imagine for me a little boy about your own age, with shaggy dark hair and eyes so wide they seemed as if they could swallow the whole world.

His name was Arthur. Arthur Toolings, but all his friends called him Tootles.

He was the first child the Reaper took.

What happened? Ah, well, you see…

Arthur often stayed up late at night, sitting at his open window. One such night, he gazed up at the stars, and imagined a place made just for him. His young soul had been filled with horrors, leaving just enough room for a single wish: to fly away to the stars.

On that particular night, he must have drifted off, for when he looked back up, there was someone perched on his windowsill—*oh, yes, exactly like I'm doing now, in fact.*

It was a boy. A boy with piercing green eyes and ruffled, pale hair that looked as though the wind had played in it just moments before. Crimson leaves clung to his worn gray coat.

He was the Reaper, though Tootles did not know it.

"Hello!" the Reaper said.

"Hello?" Tootles scrunched his forehead. "Who are you?"

"Oh." The Reaper waved a dismissive hand. "No one, really."

Tootles did know, however, that everyone was somebody. When he promptly said so, a grin spread across the Reaper's face. "I suppose you could say I'm a Storyteller of sorts." The moon behind him cast a strange shadow over his features, cloaking him in darkness.

"A Storyteller?" Tootles repeated flatly. He imagined one of the simpleton bards down at the tavern, yodeling on about some lost love or pirate treasure.

"Yes," the Reaper replied. "Uh, what's wrong with your face?"

Tootles, despite his best effort, could not wipe the look of disgust from his expression. "It just seems dumb, being a Storyteller."

The Reaper vaulted off the windowsill, and landed on the ground with a thump. He drew himself up with an offended air. "Storytelling is not dumb. Particularly the kind *I* do."

"And what kind is that?" Tootles asked. He had only ever heard of one kind of story, you see. And that was the kind told by cruel-hearted people, meant to boast or terrify or simply make noise. Nothing, surely, worth hearing.

"The stories *I* tell help make the world better," the Reaper said. "They change fate. Shift reality to something better. Something... safe."

The empty hole inside Tootles, the place that would be filled by his wish if it were ever fulfilled, began to gnaw with hunger.

"Then tell me one," Tootles said. "Tell me a story."

And the Reaper did.

As the Reaper spun his story, Tootles could *see* it. Another world grew up along the rotting boards of his small room. Vibrant, green life exploded from the floor, brushing his legs with pink flower petals and grass blades as soft as a blanket. Laughing voices, lilting songs, and faint, glimmering figures danced in through the window on shadowed feet—bringing with them an encompassing sense of joy. And for a fleeting moment, Tootles thought that perhaps tonight was the night his wish would be fulfilled.

But, as all stories must, it came to an end.

As the Reaper fell silent, and the story faded back into the worn walls, he reached out and took Tootle's small, starved hand—*just like this*—and he looked him straight in the eye. "I'm going to take you away somewhere safe," he told him. "You won't have to face the pain that awaits you in the future."

And just like that, *dear listener,* Tootles simply ceased to exist.

Shhh, it's okay little one. Don't be scared. I'm not going to hurt you, all right? It won't hurt at all. I'm sorry. Just close your eyes. In another heartbeat, you'll no longer exist.

NEVER LOOKING DOWN

Jade La Grange

Winds bellow up high
against the night sky
as I view my town too far beneath
for my feet to even scrape
Finite in its form
Too fixed into place
Too much... like a shadow

Instead, I find my hands
caress the clouds
stroke the stars
hold the heavens
as I ride its celestial currents
alongside the silhouette
of an actual shooting star
Neither a plane
nor a bird

and far more of a hero to me
than anyone could ever be

This wish of a boy
is leading me towards a place that's
Never-ending
in happiness
Never-lacking
in fun
Never-empty
of magic
Turbulent troubles, worrisome woes
are to return
Nevermore
I guess that's why they call it Neverland
Everything that I've come to know...

...will Never be again

PETER AND THE NEVER GIRL

Tasha Kazanjian

London, 1980

I **'M BORED."**

Peter glanced at Nikki. His little sister lay on her stomach, stretched out across the bar, with her arms folded under her chin. She stuck out her lower lip and whined, "Nothing *interesting* happens during the day. Why's the pub even open?"

"So we can take money from day drinkers," Peter replied.

Nikki rolled her eyes. "But there aren't any here. Can't we just close up and go somewhere? I'm *bored*."

"C'mon, you know Jamie would sack me if I left in the middle of my shift. He might put up with a lot of crap, but he won't stand for that." Pulling a mug down from the shelf, Peter set it near Nikki's head. "Here, I've got a game for you." He gave the mug an expert shove, and it streaked across the worn wood of the bar.

Nikki jolted as the mug sped towards her face, but of course, it sailed right through her transparent body, the glint of the glass just visible.

"Very funny," she said sarcastically as Peter laughed. "Aren't you tired of that one yet?"

"Nah," Peter grinned. "You jump every time."

Shrugging, Nikki sat up and crossed her legs. "So would you, if someone threw a mug at your face."

Peter began wiping down the bar for the tenth time that hour. "Except that it can't hurt you." He tried to keep the comment light, but there was an edge of bitterness to it. Quickly, he added, "You'd think you'd get used to the whole ghost thing after five years."

"I'm not a *ghost*," Nikki retorted, the way he knew she would. Before she could scold him any further, though, the door slammed open.

A girl marched in, her heels stomping across the beer-sticky floor. A guy caught the door just before it swung shut and shouldered through. He reached out to grab the girl's arm and she jerked away, crossing her arms and hunching into her oversize leather jacket. Her dark hair, teased into a frizzy cloud, almost crackled with annoyance.

Peter reckoned if she got any madder she'd start sending off sparks, and the whole hair-sprayed mess would go up in smoke.

"Piss off," she said flatly.

"Don't be like that, Dawn," the guy said, grinning.

Peter eyed him. He knew the type—the sort of idiot who thought he was tough just because he had holes in his jeans and a ring in his ear. This one looked like a skinhead with his combat boots and shaved hair.

The guy shrugged and shoved his thumbs in his pockets. "All right, so I was an idiot. Just let me walk you home."

"No. *Thanks*." She stalked to the bar and plunked down on one of the stools.

Nikki smirked at Peter who raised an eyebrow in return. Finally, a bit of entertainment.

The guy followed the girl, resting his elbows on the counter. He tilted his head to meet her eyes. "If you wanted a drink, you could've told me."

"I'm not getting a drink," she said acidly, and then turned to Peter. "You serve coffee?"

They did not serve coffee, but Peter nodded.

"No, they don't," the guy said. He shot Peter a menacing look. "Look, Dawn, it's just us and the barkeep. This place isn't even open, is it?" He gestured around the room.

"If it wasn't open, why would we leave the door unlocked?" Nikki countered.

It was a good point, and since he was the only one who could hear her, Peter opened his mouth to repeat it. Before he could get a word out, the guy smacked his hand down on the bar and said, "Stop making a scene, Dawn. It's embarrassing."

"I said *piss off*, Jim."

The guy—Jim—grabbed Dawn's shoulder, spinning her around to face him. "What do you want, an apology? All I did was try to kiss you." He smiled and ran his hand up her arm. "It isn't like I haven't done that before."

Dawn hit him.

In his line of work, Peter saw plenty of violent disagreements. He considered himself something of an expert on the subject, in fact. What surprised him about this one was that Dawn didn't hit Jim's face or even his stomach. She punched him in the arm, just above his elbow.

Even more surprising was Jim's howl of pain.

Peter stared at the pair. Dawn hunched her shoulders and glared at Jim, who clutched his arm, grimacing.

"You *bitch*," he growled as he leaned towards her. Dawn drew back her fist, ready to strike again, but Jim grabbed her wrist and twisted it hard. She cried out.

Whoever this girl was, Peter reckoned she wasn't helpless. At least, she knew enough about fighting to aim for a pressure point rather than the face. Still, Jim was twice her size and howling mad.

And besides, Peter wasn't one to miss out on a fight.

He gripped the edge of the bar and swung himself over, feet first. His trainers landed in Jim's ribs. The guy staggered, his grip on Dawn's arm broken. He gasped for air and whirled around.

Peter dropped to the ground in a crouch and straightened, his thumbs in his pockets. "I can see you have a plentiful lack of wit, since there's really only one meaning to the phrase *piss off*. So I'll keep this simple: leave now, or I'll beat you shitless."

Jim's mouth twisted into a snarl. "Stay out of it, or you're the one who—"

Before he could finish the threat, Peter punched him in the mouth. Jim's head whipped to one side. He stumbled but caught himself. Blood on his chin, he lurched forward and slammed his fist into Peter's face.

White hot pain sparked in Peter's head and scorched his sight. Momentarily blinded, he barely managed to keep his balance. "Bloody, bawdy *bastard*," he spat, the words rimmed with blood. He lowered his shoulders, ready for the next bout.

The skinhead was bigger than him, broad-shouldered and bull-headed, and he had the mottled nose and purpled knuckles of a bruiser. Still, Peter was quick—and dirty. This man fought for an audience; Peter fought to win by any means necessary. He feinted, dodged Jim's fist, and ducked behind him, jamming a strategic elbow into the skinhead's lower back. Jim twisted and let out a groan of pain.

"That," Peter said, scarcely out of breath, "was your kidney. So don't panic when you start pissing blood. Had enough yet?"

Howling, Jim charged towards him.

"Fly, Peter!" Nikki yelled.

He was already in the air. The ceiling of the pub was low, criss-crossed with old, splintering support beams. With one good jump, Peter caught hold of a beam and pulled himself up into the rafters. Jim, barreling towards him, wrapped his arms around empty air. Peter winked at Nikki, then pitched down onto the skinhead's back.

Jim hit the ground and let out a strangled gasp, the wind clearly knocked out of him. Peter, on top of him, felt the fall reverberate through his own bones but kept his breath steady. In a second, he was back on his feet, his fists clenched around the skinhead's collar. Peter hauled him towards the door, yanked it open, and shoved him out onto the street.

The bell jingled pleasantly as the door slammed shut again.

"Still want that coffee?" Peter asked Dawn, striding back towards the bar.

She stared at him, her mouth half open. Then her lips slid into a smile, and she shrugged. "Yeah, why not."

The only coffeepot in the whole pub was back in the kitchen, a battered old Poly Perk. The electric percolator with its cheerful daisy print looked a bit ridiculous there, surrounded by dirty tankards and empty beer bottles. Peter tipped some grounds into the filter and waited for it to bubble.

"What are you doing?" Nikki hissed.

Peter glanced up at her. She'd gotten down from the bar and poked her head into the kitchen, her long blonde hair falling into her face.

"We don't serve coffee," she added.

"I know," Peter replied. "But I reckon that idiot's still mooching around the street, so she's not about to leave, and I don't think she'll buy a real drink. Might as well charge her for *something*."

Nikki wrinkled her nose, but the coffeepot emitted a low grumble and Peter turned away to search for an appropriate cup. There were only two real coffee mugs in the kitchen—one belonging to him and one belonging to Jamie. Peter opted for a glass beer mug instead. He filled it almost to the brim with coffee and brought it back out into the main room.

Dawn had pulled a compact and a lipstick out of her purse. She held the mirror up to her face, running the color back and forth over her lips. Peter watched her narrowly as he set the glass down on the bar. She seemed oddly focused, given that she'd applied the color at least three times already. Until he realized that the mirror, if she angled it right, would give her a good look out onto the street.

She could've just turned around, Peter thought. But then, of course, she might look worried.

"So where'd you pick him up?" he asked, jerking a thumb at the door.

"Probably a police station," Nikki muttered. She'd taken her seat on top of the bar again.

Peter fought back a grin.

Dawn tugged on the bow in her hair. "There's this cellar, down by the Langdon Park station, where they've got fights every weekend. Mostly skinheads, but my friend Carole has a cousin, Derek, who runs the bets. Anyway, my other friend, Lynda—she's mad about Derek. So we went. Jim's always there—he's one of the best, has a *mean* right hook—"

"Hang on," Peter interrupted.

"What?"

"I don't actually care."

With half an exasperated laugh, Dawn snapped her compact shut. "All right. Here's a question for you, then. Why'd you fight him?"

"Don't like idiots in my pub, that's all," Peter replied.

"Is it your pub?"

Nikki snorted. "Might as well be, seeing as Jamie makes you do all the work."

That wasn't quite fair, but Peter couldn't argue with her while Dawn sat there. He'd look insane. "It's not *my* pub, exactly," he said. "But I can still run idiots off the place. He's gone, by the way."

Dawn didn't turn to look, though her shoulders relaxed slightly. "I'll take that coffee now."

Peter gave the glass a push to slide down the counter. Dawn caught it, but coffee sloshed over the rim and spilled onto her fingerless leather gloves. She winced, shaking her hands so little drops sprayed everywhere, and gave Peter a glare.

Nikki responded by sticking out her tongue.

Dawn stuck out hers, too.

Nikki's eyes widened while Peter stiffened. "You—"

"What? She started it." Dawn took a swig of her coffee. Red lipstick stained the glass.

Swallowing, Peter found his voice. "You can see her?"

At that, Dawn tensed. "Yes," she said, drawing out the word. Her gaze shifted to Nikki, then back to Peter. "I can see a lot of things."

A chill twined through Peter's blood. He stared at her, his hands clenched around the edge of the counter. Five years. It'd been five years since . . . since Nikki. And in all that time, he'd never met anyone else who could see her, nor had he ever told anyone she existed. They'd think he was insane or tripping. They'd try to drug him out of it, or detox him out of it, or just talk him out of it. By the time they were done, he damn well *would* be insane. It would kill Nikki—well, kill her all over again—to watch.

He knew there were people who *would* believe him, who claimed that they could see spirits, too. But that was a load of crap, because none of them could see Nikki. She could run circles around them all day, and they wouldn't even get goose pimples.

Except this girl. This girl looked right at Nikki, studying her carefully.

Peter swallowed. "What do you mean, you can see a lot of things? Like other ghosts?"

"Ghosts?"

"Yeah, like Nikki. Are you some kind of psychic?"

"Ghosts and psychics," she snorted. "And here I thought you were clever, quoting Hamlet in a fight."

Peter's mouth quirked. "You caught that?"

"'Bloody, bawdy villain?'" Dawn cocked her head and continued the line. "'Remorseless, treacherous, lecherous, kindless villain.' You had him pegged, all right. But there are more things in heaven and earth, Horatio, than are dreamt of in your philosophy."

"It's Peter, actually," he said, crossing his arms. "So tell me what it is on heaven and earth that I haven't dreamt about."

"D'you have any biscuits?" Dawn asked.

"Not that I've dreamed about lately."

She rolled her eyes. "I mean in the kitchen. I'm hungry."

"She's lying," Nikki said suddenly.

"No, really, I'm *starved*," Dawn replied. "I haven't eaten all day."

Nikki stood up and fixed her hands on her hips. "It doesn't matter if she can see me. She doesn't know anything."

With a slight smile, Dawn took a sip of her coffee. "You might want to hear me out first. Before calling me a liar."

"Peter," Nikki hissed. "*Don't*. Just kick her out now."

He turned around and disappeared into the kitchen, returning a moment later with a pack of digestives. "Ok," he said as he set them down in front of Dawn. "So what is it you see?"

Dawn opened the package, wrestled out a biscuit, and dunked it in the coffee. "Souls," she said through a mouthful of crumbs. "I see souls."

Peter clawed his fingers through his tangle of ginger hair. "How's that different from ghosts?"

"Because, idiot, a soul isn't necessarily a ghost," Dawn said, jamming the rest of the biscuit in her mouth. "*You've* got a soul. Bit of a mess, honestly, but it's there."

"You're telling me that you can see my soul?" Peter said.
She nodded.

His mouth twisted into a skeptical smile. "What's it look like?"

Dawn looked at him. Her eyes gleamed—a bit like the edge of a knife. They were a strange color, a pale grey-green. Peter wanted to blink, pull himself out of that gaze, but he couldn't.

Then Dawn smiled and continued as though he hadn't asked a question at all. "I know there are all kinds of stories about ghosts—like *Hamlet*—but souls don't actually hang around. They go where they're going, and that's that. Souls on this earth are always attached to a body. I see them every single day, all the time." She turned her bright eyes on Nikki again. "But I've never seen one on its own before."

"I guess I'm special," Nikki smirked.

Peter slouched across the bar and shook his head. "Hang on. You're saying that Nik's the only ghost you've ever seen?"

"*Not* a ghost," Dawn and Nikki said at the same time.

The girls stared at each other. Nikki glowered while Dawn arched an eyebrow and added, "She's not."

"So what am I, smart-arse?" Nikki stood up, stuck her hands on her hips, and glared down at the other girl. "Just what do you think I am?"

Dawn took another sip of coffee. "What do *you* think you are?"

At that, there was silence.

Not a ghost. It was an old joke, like the lines of a play memorized beyond all meaning. It *had* to become a joke, because the first time Nikki said it, Peter thought his own soul was being ripped in half. He'd sat huddled on the pavement in front of a charity shop, surrounded by a squall of blue and red light—the flashing beams of police cars reflected in greasy puddles and shattered glass. A nightmare so vivid he couldn't pretend to be asleep, trapped in the awful reality of sensation: the smell of sour beer and chips frying, the crackle of radios and low voices.

And then Nikki, right beside him, asking why he looked so sick.

Ghost. It was the only word he'd been able to say. And Nikki hadn't liked it much.

But he'd never asked what else she might be. He reckoned she just wanted to pretend, and it didn't matter, anyway. Whatever she was, she was real.

Now, Dawn asked again, "What *are* you?"

"I'm me," Nikki said shortly. "Nicola Mabel Isen. And I belong with Peter."

Dawn shrugged. Her leather jacket fell off her shoulders, though she kept her arms halfway in the sleeves. She didn't look like a skinhead, Peter noticed, not with those clothes and that frizzing cloud of hair. Under the jacket, she had on a blue floral dress with a wide collar. A gold charm winked from a chain around her neck—a thimble, Peter realized.

He also realized, as she sat there with her head cocked to one side and her lips curled into a maddening kind of smile, that he was staring at her and didn't want to stop.

Her gaze, however, fixed on Nikki. "Belong?" she repeated quietly. "No, Nikki, you don't belong here at all."

"Hang on a mo," Peter said. His chest tightened. "How do you know where she belongs? So what if you've never seen a soul like her before? If she's stayed behind, it's because she's supposed to be here."

Nikki nodded triumphantly. "Exactly. I can't leave Peter."

Dawn turned to Peter now, shifting closer to him. "Listen, Horatio, what was that ghost in *Hamlet* doing up there on the parapet? He was telling his son to hurry up and avenge him because he was *trapped*. Forget about all those idiots trying to chat with the dead. The dead aren't talking. They're meant to go where they go, and that's final. A soul still here, when the body's long gone—that isn't right. Not for you, and not for her."

"Don't tell him what's right for me," Nikki interjected. She stomped her foot on the bar. "I told you, I'm right where I'm supposed to be."

Peter reached out to Nikki, a placating gesture, though he kept his eyes on Dawn. "Are you trying to say I'm supposed to avenge her?" A vicious, bitter kind of pain spasmed in his gut. He wanted to shock her, see the look of horror on her face. "That might be hard, seeing as I'm the one who killed her."

Dawn flushed and went very still. "How?"

"It wasn't your fault," Nikki said angrily. She jumped off the bar—she fell just as fast as any ordinary kid, only there was no thud of her feet hitting the ground—and ran over to Peter. "It *wasn't*. You tried to stop me."

He wanted to grab her shoulders, but that was useless. Instead, he jammed his hands in his pockets and muttered, "It doesn't matter. No changing what happened now."

"And what happened, exactly?" Dawn asked.

"What, worried you ought to be calling the police?" Peter said as carelessly as he could. He turned his back on her and began cleaning the glasses behind the bar.

"No." Dawn's voice was very soft now. "You're forgetting that I can see your soul, too."

He stiffened.

"You're not a murderer, Peter. Whatever happened."

What do you know about it? The retort stung in his throat, but he couldn't speak; her words seemed to tear into his chest, somehow burning and numbing all at once. Like vodka poured on a wound. Peter remembered that sensation vividly.

When he was twelve, he'd fallen off his bike. The gravel ground his leg to a pulp. Nikki—seven at the time and luckily the only one home—climbed up onto the counter and grabbed a bottle of vodka from the cabinet. She'd read it in a book, she said. They had to disinfect the wound.

If Peter hadn't been so dizzy from the pain, he would've told her it was mad. Not because it would hurt like hell, but because their father would kill them for wasting vodka. He didn't have the strength to protest, though, not until she dumped the alcohol onto his leg. Then he screamed bloody murder, but soon the pain faded into a warm, almost gentle ache.

He could almost feel the old scars on his leg burning now. Peter realized he hadn't taken a breath since Dawn spoke, and he sucked in a thin gulp of air. He wanted her strange eyes off him, wanted to be alone with Nikki again. Still, a thread of something feather-shy and yet so damned *strong* pulled him towards this girl, begging for her to keep talking.

Dawn pushed away the empty glass and stood up. "I can help you, if you let me. Call it a thank you for kicking Jim's arse. But I can't do anything unless you tell me what happened." She waited a moment, then shrugged and turned to go.

"Wait," Peter said quickly.

Nikki let out a huff of surprise.

"We ran away," he added. The words sounded so simple, so easy, as if the memories didn't have him wrapped up in barbed wire. "Or I did. I told her she couldn't come, said if she did, I'd bring her right back to Dad. I meant to get to London and find a job of some kind—I was fourteen, but I could pass as older. Nikki snuck onto the train with me, only I didn't realize it. Once I got to the city, I didn't know where I was going, didn't know Nikki was following me. She planned to stay out of sight until I settled down somewhere for the night, but something scared her. She ran after me, yelling, and I turned around to see her bolting across the street—"

He stopped there. The next words should've been simple: *There was a lorry.* But he couldn't say them.

"So?" Nikki said, spinning around to face Dawn. "You going to magically *fix it* now? Well, you can't. He needs me, and I'm not leaving him, not ever! You can't make me." She lifted her chin, a glint of white fire in her blue eyes. "Even death couldn't make me."

Even though Peter knew he couldn't touch her, in that moment, she seemed truly *real*. Solid. Alive. Her words rang like a threat, and he wondered if Dawn could feel it, too—that spark of power. Maybe that's what first convinced him Nikki wasn't a hallucination. He couldn't touch her, but he could feel her presence, feel her laughter and her taunts and her temper. All of it flooded the air that he breathed like dust.

His spitfire little sister, who told death to go to hell just because she wanted to stay with him.

Whoever Dawn was, whatever strange power she had, Peter reckoned she was no match for Nikki.

"I can't magically fix anything." Dawn directed her words to Peter, not Nikki. "I told you, I'm not a psychic. But I think I can help."

Peter arched an eyebrow. She was persistent; he'd give her that. With a shrug, he cleared away the empty glass and the biscuits. "You heard her. She doesn't want to go. So I reckon this isn't *Hamlet* after all, and we don't need any help." He grinned at Nikki. "Right?"

"Right!"

"You're just one-of-a-kind, is all," he said, winking at her.

Nikki sniffed. "I already knew that."

"And that's fifty pence for the coffee." Peter held out his hand to Dawn, palm up. "Plus extra for the biscuits."

Dawn's mouth pinched, then flared into a smile. She tugged her jacket back onto her shoulders and dug around in the pockets. "Sorry. I don't have any money on me. Jim promised to pay the bill."

She sauntered over to the door, ignoring Peter's "*Oy!*" as she pulled it open. The bell jingled overhead. "If you want to collect," she called, "you can always come to Roger's, down in Langdon Park."

The door thudded shut behind her.

Shadowed.

That was what Peter's soul looked like. Shadowed. A thumb smudged over a pencil drawing or the cloudy, mascara-speckled streaks left behind after you had a cry.

Dawn scraped a tear away with one nail and paused to inspect herself in a shop window. She barely knew which part of Poplar she was in, except that she must be close to the river because she could smell it. Her stupid shoes hurt, her legs were cold, the smell of hairspray made her sick—and now she had a slime of damp mascara around her eyes.

Her mother used to say tears were just a side-effect of seeing souls. "They aren't pretty, darling, not most of them." Mum had liked pretty things, Dawn thought wryly. They still had bits and dregs of HP—hired purchase—furniture, though it was all battered and long out of fashion by now. And yet they *still* didn't own it.

Mum had left several years earlier. Dawn could forgive her for that, because at least there were fewer bills to sort. Jack, the oldest, took it harder, though he'd never admitted it.

Souls weren't pretty; Dawn could agree with Mum on that much. Film stars were pretty. The window displays at Marks & Spencer were pretty. Carole's latest shade of lipstick was very pretty, and Dawn still meant to ask her where she'd gotten it. But souls were something else entirely.

It wasn't Peter's soul that made her cry—not exactly. At least she hadn't cried in front of him, though when he started talking about what happened to Nikki, she'd felt a hard knot of heat in her throat and had to swallow it back. She wanted to ask him what they ran away *from* and what happened to him after Nikki died. She wanted to reach out and somehow take on some of the pain clear in his voice, in the tension of his muscles, in the sharp edge of his smile.

Dawn fumbled with the zipper of her jacket—Jack's old jacket, actually—and then turned away from the window. She looked a mess, but there wasn't anything she could do about it now. The first order of business was to find a chip shop. Her stomach growled, the biscuits and coffee already a fading memory.

There was a nice, greasy little place near the waterfront. Dawn got herself a paper-wrapped package of fish and chips, plunked herself down on a bench, and began to eat. A brutal March wind skimmed off the Thames. She tucked her legs underneath her and savored the scalding heat of the food. Peter created enough of a problem on his own, she thought, dunking a chip in brown sauce, but then there was Nikki.

There was something very wrong with Nikki's soul.

It wasn't that Dawn could read minds or anything nearly so useful. *After all, if I could've seen what was on Jim's mind, I wouldn't have gone out with him*, she thought grimly. Souls weren't nearly as straightforward as thoughts. Even in Jim's soul, Dawn could see glints and echoes of a different sort of man altogether—courage instead of bravado, kindness instead of charm. She could see, vaguely, the sketch of the man he was meant to be, though the lines had gone crooked. So she'd said yes when he asked her out the night before, but once he had her alone, she quickly realized just how crooked those lines had become.

Dawn slathered another chip in brown sauce and gulped it down before any could drip on her sleeves. Peter, for all the shadows, didn't seem anything like Jim. If nothing else, Dawn smirked to herself, he was a damn sight better at fighting.

But Nikki.

The sketch of Nikki's soul was so very blurred and all tangled up with Peter's. Dawn could scarcely tell where Nikki ended and Peter began. Which made sense, if Nikki wanted so badly to stay with him that she'd somehow cheated death itself. Except that death, as far as Dawn had seen, couldn't be cheated.

She crumpled up the empty paper and chucked it in a bin, then started towards home. Her little brother, Mike, would be angry with her for staying out so long; she ought to pick him up a comic or a Mars bar with the last few pence in her pocket.

Naturally she'd lied to Peter about not having money. But she wanted to see him again, and Roger's seemed like a decent idea at the time. Mike would miss her if she went out again, though, and she couldn't blame him. He needed her. He'd given her such puppy eyes when she left with Carole and Lynda the night before. Her friends had dragged her to Roger's and swept her up in a delicious swirl of vodka and freedom, until she felt like just another eighteen-year-old, wearing uncomfortable heels and flirting with a boy. Of course, her date with Jim hadn't exactly turned out the way she'd hoped, but it brought her to Peter.

Which meant she *had* to go to the club again tonight. Just in case he came looking for her.

Roger's. Peter had never heard of that club before.

Then again, it wasn't as though he paid attention. Most of the pub regulars talked a lot, especially after a drink—complaints about their jobs, their families, or that Thatcher woman and her damn policies—but Peter only listened to Nikki's commentary on the crowd. Her snarky comments usually had him biting the inside of his lip to keep a straight face. Every once in a while, when he could get away with it, he'd mutter something back.

Tonight, though, he wasn't listening. Nikki could tell and went into a sulk, nearly disappearing entirely. She climbed up on top of a cabinet and crouched there like a baleful housecat, even more transparent than usual. Only her blue eyes glittered in the darkness. For once, she *did* look like a spook, and Peter avoided turning around. Instead, he leaned across the bar and let the cheerful roar of conversation fill his ears.

Jamie's pub, the Bereford Arms, was a typical corner affair; each evening, everyone on the street stopped by for a brew. It wasn't the sort of place where teenagers congregated, not skins or mods or those weird ruffles-and-eyeliner kids who liked David Bowie. No one caused any trouble—or at least, the same people always caused the same trouble. Everything ran like clockwork.

"Another round here, mate," a man at the bar called.

Peter poured the drink and shoved it towards the man without looking up. A second later, he heard a smash and a string of curses.

"What the hell d'you think you're doing?" the man yelled. Ale soaked his shirt, and he glared at Peter. "Bloody idiot!"

Peter crossed his arms and retorted, "Sorry, I didn't realize you were too sloshed to catch it."

The man's eyebrows went up, and he stood, fists clenched. Before he could do anything, though, Jamie popped in from the kitchen. He hurried over to the bar and apologized to the patron, one hand behind his back to shoo Peter away.

Happy to escape from both the furious man and Nikki's glare, Peter complied. He slipped through the kitchen, which reeked of burnt coffee and sour beer, and went out into the back alley. He needed air.

Spirals of wind sent bits of paper twirling through the air. Each gust smelled of something different—cigarette smoke, then perfume, then river water, then chips, then curry powder from the Indian restaurant next door. Peter wanted to chase after the wind's tail and leave the pub behind.

Leave Nikki behind. Just for the night.

She hadn't any right to be so sullen, he thought. Hadn't he sent Dawn packing? It had always been just the two of them, Peter and

Nikki against the world, and that wasn't about to change because a pretty girl turned his head.

Still, he wanted to see Dawn again. Only because he wanted to *see* her, not because he wanted her help. He would ask her how she'd come to memorize insults from Shakespeare and where she'd gone on her date with that wanker Jim—well, that was the wanker's first problem, wasn't it? That was the worst date spot in Canary Wharf (ask anyone you like), and if *he* was going to take her somewhere—

It'd be easy enough to charm her, to make her smile. Peter wanted to see that slightly teasing smile again.

And Nikki was being a pest.

Jamie wouldn't mind if he took the night off. At least, not if he was back by midnight and did a bit of groveling and all the washing up.

Peter let the wind shut the kitchen door and started towards the street. Roger's, she'd said, down in Langdon Park. Less than half an hour's walk away.

"Where are you going?" someone said behind him.

He cursed and spun around.

It was Nikki, her arms crossed. She didn't shiver, despite her thin sweater and faded summer dress. The wind, which whipped Peter's jacket and tousled hair, couldn't touch her. "Where are you going?" she repeated.

"Out to have some fun, is all," Peter said, turning away again.

"Without me?" Nikki hissed.

"I thought you were sulking," Peter replied. "So go on and sulk. I'll be back in a few hours."

She half-ran to keep up with his long strides. "I'm *not* sulking! You're the one who went all quiet and grumpy. And how can you have any fun if I'm not with you?" She tossed her pigtails back and started skipping. "Where are we going, then?"

Peter stopped. "*You're* not coming."

Nikki's eyes widened. "But . . . but that's not right." She shook her head vigorously. "That's not how this works."

"It's how it's working tonight," Peter retorted. "I said go on. Give me a night off, will you? I want to be alone."

Her face went blank with shock. Peter felt a sharp stab of guilt in his gut. He grimaced, wishing he could take the words back, and opened his mouth to say he didn't mean it.

But then Nikki's eyes flashed. "You're going to see that girl."

Peter's remorse vanished. "So what if I am?" he shot back.

"You can't!"

A cold, stubborn kind of anger zizzed in his blood. "Can't? I can do whatever I bloody well like, Nik, with or without you." As he strode away, he almost expected her to appear in front of him, but she only called his name.

He ignored her.

Peter found Roger's easily enough. He only had to follow a group of skins stumbling their way down Chrisp Street, and they led him right to it: a brick building with warped glass windows and a formidable old door. Music throbbed as the gang of teenagers yanked the door open, and Peter darted in behind them.

He found himself swept into a crowd, swallowed whole by movement and music and smoke. Glasses clanked against each other as people tried to move, the place cramped and low-ceilinged. Peter kept to the edges in order to move around the throng and shifted from one room to the next. There were several, all of them packed. He found the bar and ordered a pint, then drifted along with the mob until he spotted a narrow staircase. A brawny skin lounged at the bottom, his arms crossed.

A guard, Peter decided. That was where he needed to go. He shoved and elbowed his way out of the mob, his beer disappearing somewhere along the way, and finally reached the stairs. Shouts rained down from the top. The brawny skin shifted to block Peter's view and glowered at him.

"Shove up, then," Peter said and jerked his chin towards the stairs. "I'm late for a date."

"You got an invitation?" the skin asked.

Peter grinned. "Sure. I told you, I've got a date. And I'm an old friend of Jim's."

The skin eyed him for a moment. Then he grunted and stepped aside. Peter clapped the skin on the back as he sauntered past.

Upstairs, there was only one large room, empty of furniture and stuffed with bodies. Everyone crammed up against the walls to create a clear space for two brawling men, both of them stripped to the waist and already sporting bruises. Peter eyed them critically. Showy, he decided. Definitely no hitting below the belt. More palatable for spectators that way.

Neither of them was Jim, Peter noticed. The bastard still might be hanging around somewhere—not that Peter cared. The real problem was that he hadn't spotted Dawn. She wasn't part of the cheering and jeering onlookers, and he hadn't seen her downstairs, either. Strange, how much the disappointment pinched. Peter frowned, aggravated with himself. He should just go back to Jamie's, he thought, turning towards the stairs.

And found himself face to face with her.

She stood at the top of the steps, clinging to the arm of another girl. Though she wore the same leather jacket, she'd traded her dress for a skirt and jumper. Her heels tripped over the last step as she locked eyes with Peter.

He grinned. "Fancy seeing you here. You still owe me a quid."

Unfortunately, a sudden howl from the spectators drowned out the quip. Peter glanced over his shoulder to see that one of the brawlers on the ground and the other with his fists raised in triumph. A scrawny skin wearing a Union Jack t-shirt entered the makeshift ring. He clapped the victor on the back and yelled something to the crowd. Peter turned back to Dawn.

She smiled.

Her friend tugged on her sleeve, and Dawn whispered something in her ear. The other girl's eyes widened with alarm but Dawn reached out and grabbed Peter's arm, pulling him into the staircase.

"Go on, Carole, I'll catch up," Dawn said. After a moment's hesitation, her friend disappeared into the crowd. Several other people rushed up the staircase just then. As Peter moved to let them pass, he found himself pressed up against Dawn. Her hand tightened around his arm.

With their faces so close together, they didn't have to yell. "I didn't think you'd come," Dawn said.

Peter shrugged. "I'm full of surprises."

Dawn peered around him, then down the steps. "Where's Nikki?"

"I told her to take the night off," Peter replied, noticing how Dawn's eyebrows shot up. "I wanted to talk to you. Alone."

"Oh?" Dawn's mouth quirked, and she crossed her arms. "So you're not just here to collect the bill?"

He could've said yes. He could've teased her or made a joke. Except that he could see a gleam of uncertainty in her expression. She stood on the brink of the step as though poised to take flight at any moment. He *had* to say something to keep her there.

"I told her to stay behind tonight," he said quickly. "I've never done that before. I didn't even know if it would work." He rubbed the back of his neck, choosing his next words a bit more carefully. "She's a stubborn kid. But she didn't follow me here, and I think . . . look, I just wanted to know what you thought. About all this. About what I should do, because maybe I *could* do something, if it's true that Nikki shouldn't be here."

"It is true." Dawn leaned forward. "Peter, I meant what I said. Something's wrong. I'm sure of it."

"How can you be so sure?" Peter asked, unable to stop himself. Her insistence still sounded like an accusation.

Another couple shouldered past them, and Dawn grimaced. "Look, we can't talk here." She grasped his hand and tugged him down the stairs with her.

Peter didn't resist, but before they reached the bottom, he heard a shout from behind them.

"Dawn!"

She tensed and slowly turned around. Her grip on Peter's hand loosened, but he didn't let go. Instead, he knotted his fingers into hers and slouched against the wall, his head tilted back so he could see the man on the steps above them. "Hello again, Jim," he said with a smile.

"*You.*" Jim folded his arms and glared at them. His shoulders seemed to fill the doorway. "Dawn, get away from this prick."

Dawn snorted. "Oh, he's the prick?"

"You made a mistake, coming here," Jim growled. "You're on my patch now, and I'll—"

"You'll what?" Peter interrupted. "Get your arse beaten again?"

Jim's mouth curled into a snarl. He thundered down the steps and snatched the front of Peter's shirt.

Peter's hand tore out of Dawn's as the skinhead hauled him away. Dawn staggered, nearly losing her balance. Peter wrenched his neck around as he tried to keep sight of her. Those stupid shoes—she would fall down the stairs.

Dawn managed to catch herself, collapsing against the wall. One of her high heels bounced down the steps. Peter writhed against Jim's grip and reached out to her, and then the skin's fist landed in his face.

Light erupted behind Peter's eyes. He sagged, vaguely aware of Jim lugging him up the stairs. Just as his vision began to clear, the skin threw him to the ground in the center of the room.

Blood dripped from Peter's nose and he spat out a cough, rolling onto his side. Jim's boot caught him in the ribs, once, then again and again. Peter curled into a ball. Pain spasmed through his chest and petrified his lungs.

Bloody, bawdy bastard. This skin damn well wanted him dead, Peter realized.

Distantly, he could hear the clamor of the crowd. A girl's voice stood out, a cry that cut through the din. Jim kept kicking. Peter gritted his teeth and forced himself to move. He had to do something *quick* or he was done for.

With a grunt, he flipped onto his back, braced his hands behind his head, and swung his foot up between Jim's legs.

It sure as hell wasn't cricket, but it did the trick. The mob around them booed as Jim groaned and doubled over. Peter, his torso still throbbing with pain, didn't hesitate. He launched himself at Jim. One hand clenched around the skin's collar, Peter kneed Jim in his side and then punched him repeatedly in the ear.

The rabble pressed in closer now. Peter's eyes flashed at them. Jim had been right about one thing: this was his patch and Peter reckoned he was in for it even if he beat the bastard senseless. And Dawn—where was she? He caught a glimpse of her, half hidden behind a knot of shrieking girls with Chelsea cuts.

Jim wrested around and got a fist in Peter's stomach. A new crash of pain jangled up Peter's ribs, and he retaliated with a head-butt. This turned out to be a mistake. Of course the man had a skull like a cannonball.

Dizzy, Peter got a punch in the nose before he managed to kick back. This time, he hit Jim in the knee. The man crumpled to the ground.

The mob around them buzzed with a savage anger, and Peter knew he had to move while Jim was down. He darted towards Dawn and grabbed her hand. They made for the stairs, only to the way blocked by the skin who had been standing guard at the bottom.

Peter cursed.

Dawn pulled him away. "Follow me!" she shouted, pushing back into the throng. He stumbled after her. The crowd pressed in on all sides as though trying to flatten them, and Peter ducked, one arm over his head. Dawn nearly fell and he hauled her to her feet again, terrified that she'd be trampled. She clutched at him, still in the lead, and shoved them both against a wall. They paused there for a moment. Peter shifted to place himself between Dawn and the crowd, his face so close to hers that he could feel her ragged breath on his face.

"The window," Dawn hissed in his ear.

"Are you mad? How are we supposed to get down?"

"You got a better plan?" she retorted. "Besides, you're good at climbing, aren't you?"

The side of a building was a bit different from the rafters of Jamie's pub, but they were low on options. They clambered out the window.

Several skins rushed after them, and whether they meant to push them down or pull them in, Peter wasn't waiting to find out.

Crouched on the window ledge with Dawn beside him, he scanned the wall. He could see another window casing, only a meter or so down. While he wasn't sure where to go from there, it would get them away from the skins.

"Peter," Dawn whispered.

He glanced at her. She'd gone horribly pale, her fingers still tight around his arm. "Oh, *shit.* Don't tell me you're scared of heights."

"I've never really tested it before," she mumbled. "But I think I might be."

Even worse, he realized, she only had one shoe—though considering that they were heels, maybe she'd be better off without them. "Hang on to me," he said.

She looped her arms around his neck. He clutched the edge of the sill and dropped, grunting as Dawn's weight dragged him down.

His boots found the ledge beneath them, and he released the sill with one hand in order to find another hold. A moment later, they pressed up against another window, this one closed.

"It's still a long way down," Dawn said, her voice thin.

"Just shut your eyes and hold on." Peter reckoned he had to hurry, before she lost it completely—or he did. The next few moments blurred together in a haze of scrapes, bruised knees, hissed curses, and panic as he shimmied down the wall with Dawn on his back. Luckily the building was old, the bricks as gnarled as the roots of an ancient tree, and Peter found enough window ledges to guide him down. The two of them landed on the pavement, shaky and breathless.

"There they are!"

The door of Roger's burst open and a hoard of skins, led by Jim, poured out.

Peter cursed and reached for Dawn. She hesitated only long enough to pull off her remaining shoe and chuck it at Jim's head. The heel hit him between the eyes. He reeled, stunned, and one of the others had to steady him.

Peter let out a laugh, but then Jim lurched forward, his eyes fixed murderously on Dawn. She grabbed Peter's hand, and they took off.

The two of them bolted through the streets, Dawn in the lead. She weaved in and out of alleys, up metal staircases, across terraces, down and into mangy little gardens, and along a narrow spit of a river. Finally they reached the grumbling, barge-infested current of the Thames.

A pale flood of fluorescent light spilled over the deserted quay and the black water. Peter stumbled to a stop. "I think we lost them."

"*We* lost them?" Dawn said, gasping for air. She tripped over to a pillar box and braced herself against it. "I think you mean *I* lost them. You just fumbled along after me."

"Only because I was tired from climbing down the side of a building with you on my back," Peter replied, equally out of breath.

She shrugged. "Fair."

"Where are we anyway?" he asked.

Carefully, she pushed herself upright again, the movement stiff. She grimaced, her face oddly grey in the lamplight. Still half-slumped against the pillar box, she pointed to the water. "We must be around St. Katherine's. Look, you can see Tower Bridge."

Peter gawked over the water. They were miles from Poplar. Heaving a sigh, he straightened up. "Reckon we'd better get back. I've got to be at Jamie's by midnight."

Dawn nodded and turned around. She was limping, Peter noticed. A splatter of blood trailed behind her. Both of her shoes were gone now, and he winced as he realized she'd done that entire frantic dash through the city barefoot.

"Wait," he said, crouching down slightly. "Climb on. I'll give you a lift."

She hesitated, but he shook his head impatiently. "Don't be an idiot. You're bleeding."

It was easier to carry her when they *weren't* climbing down a wall, at least. As they set off, she rested her head on his shoulder and said, "I probably shouldn't have invited you there."

Peter would've shrugged, but that was hard to do with a girl on his back. "It was worth it. Just to kick that bastard in the bollocks."

He could feel Dawn's smile. "I did enjoy that," she said. "I reckon I can't go back there again, though, no matter how mad Lynda is about Derek."

"If Derek hangs around that gang, I'd say Lynda's better off without him," Peter observed.

"Fair point."

For a while, they walked in silence—or the relative silence of East London. The sound of distant cars and sirens and barge horns rose and fell with the pitch of the wind. A few other people passed them and they got one or two curious stares, but no one stopped them.

Peter's arms began to ache within a few minutes. He didn't say anything though, just trudged along and tried not to think of how sore he would be in the morning. Or what Nikki was going to say.

Once or twice he almost thought he saw her out of the corner of his eye. But it hurt to twist his neck, and each time, there was no one there.

"How do you know?" he said eventually.

Dawn shifted. "How do I know what?"

"Earlier, you said you were sure something's wrong. With Nikki, I mean." Peter wasn't even sure why he was asking. In spite of the bruises and bloody nose, everything had worked out sort of perfectly. Dawn wouldn't question his motives anymore, not after what they'd just been through—and by the way she nestled with her cheek against his neck, he reckoned this was just the beginning.

So why bring up Nikki now? Whether Dawn believed it or not, Peter knew Nikki belonged with him.

Dawn's soft sigh tickled Peter's neck. "I told you," she said. "Souls can't stay here after death, no matter how much they might want to."

"But how do you *know* that?" Peter pressed. "Nikki proves it's possible, doesn't she? If a soul wants to stay, then—"

"That isn't how it works," Dawn interrupted sharply.

Peter swallowed, annoyed.

Dawn continued before he could think up a retort. "I do know, Peter. If souls could stay just because they wanted to, then my brother would be following me around, like Nikki is following you."

Her words dropped like a weight on Peter's chest, and he slowed. Dawn slid down from his back. She stumbled over to the embankment and leaned against it, staring out over the water. Peter followed her.

"What was his name?" he asked after a pause.

"Jack." She fiddled with the zipper of her leather jacket and added, "This was his. He left it behind by accident, told me not to get too attached because he'd be taking it back when he came home for Christmas." Her chin buried in the collar, she cleared her throat. "That's what he said the last time we talked on the phone, anyway. Our mum was from Belfast, but she and Dad moved here when I was just a baby. After she took off a couple years ago—well, Jack thought she might have gone back to stay with her cousin. At least, that's what he told Dad. He said he was going to look for her. I knew it was just an excuse. He wanted to get involved."

Peter's gut wound into a knot. He didn't pay much attention to politics, but even he knew about the troubles in Ireland, especially after Lord Mountbatten's death the year before.

"He was killed last November," Dawn said, her voice very low. "Firefight. We don't even know which side did it, not that it really matters." She rubbed the heel of her hand against her cheek and then turned to look straight at Peter. Her eyes glinted with tears, her mouth a grim line. "I told you. I know, because if he could've stayed, if how much I needed him was enough to make it happen, he'd be here right now."

Peter nodded. There was nothing he could say.

And yet he still didn't believe her.

Maybe Jack hadn't wanted to stay, even if Dawn wished he would. He was gone, and she couldn't ask him. Nikki, however, was still there. Peter took that as proof enough: she wanted to be with him, and he would *never* make her leave.

But he said, "So how do we help her move on?"

"I don't know. I'll figure it out, though." She gave him a half smile. "Deal?"

That was exactly what Peter wanted to hear. "Deal." He held out his hand, and she took it. For a moment, they stood there, grinning at each other. If Peter felt a shiver of guilt about the lie, he could chalk it up to the wind blowing off the Thames.

"Right," he said as he turned around. "Get back on. It's still a long way to Poplar."

She groaned. "Do you ever wish you could fly?"

"Quit whining. You're not the one doing the work."

"Can you even carry me all the way back?" she asked.

Peter laughed. "Have a little faith, love. I'm just getting started."

The Tale Continues in Volume Two

FALLING

Brittany Eden

PETER

I wondered what space spared
Spread the inches drawn between
Sheers floating out, flowing flared
The bleeding flame, the broken frame

Our daytime star so lonely
Beneath starcast sky, lowly
Then up there where stars alight
The sun sets on lone lovely girl

Bright bright bright

For once she is unaware
my misunderstood despair
I can only stare, up there
Until the free air, the free air

Who is there? Is someone there?
She asks a window greeting
My loss and pining ending
Chosen, endless, hopeful waiting

I can breathe I can breathe I can breathe

Still lost yet somehow, she found
The question, soft perfect sound
Empty, I push down my blight
She'd see evidence of the fight

Hello? She calls in delight
My dear friend, you look a fright!
Was I that sorry a sight?
Torn shirt, disheveled hair not right

Fight fight fight

Across the rooftop, up here
The world below, I avoid
It left its mark—never, son
Never enough, to rise above

Never, never... never

It's something different up here
Her voice unlike the shouting
She moves her perch, humming near
Lifting, freedom longing clear

What's different? It's rude, my voice
Leaning past dormer window
Fearless she sings her song—*trust!*
Her precious sigh stirs dormant dust

Eternity a lit sea
Constellations like magic
Not an alley—an abyss
A single street between us

WENDY

Wide as seas, horizons weep
Black hole far—a fearsome deep
My faith and his belief a chasm
I reach across, I reach across

There's a map? He scoffs aloud
All those souls lost on the ground
I raise my eyes to the sky
Oh how I wish he—we!—could fly

Fly fly fly

Step soft, tread light, reach my hand
Please trust there's another land
Where we can fly! We can soar!
With me, you're not lost anymore

It's as easy as one two
Three steps 'til flight and far stars
Three deeper breaths but the boy
Cries: *Can your hand reach across this?*

Don't hide, please, don't hide

Swells of rising tides crying
His trusting tears like flying
Dripping shadows make a map
Dreamsky calling us up, alone

No no no

I wish I could fly, he says
I wish we could fly, I say
I can read him like a book
Something's holding him back, a hook

The Tale Continues in Volume Two

LAGOON'S EDGE

Anne J. Hill

THE MERMAID ONLY felt at home sitting on the edge of the lagoon, looking down at the reflection of her face. She couldn't see her fin that way, so she could pretend to be the legged woman she aspired to be. The one that no one else saw.

Deep down in the shimmering water, her scaly face looked back at her. She'd smile as she imagined Peter's handsome face beside her with the sky behind them. Each year, she saw him a little older—the man he'd grow into. He'd whisper sweet words into her ear, stirring the butterflies in her stomach. She'd give anything to be with Peter again.

They'd spent one summer together when they were kids. He'd trot up to the lagoon with stories to tell and sit with his feet in the water. She'd rest her chin on his knee while he played with her hair and told her about his latest victory against Hook, or something silly Tink had said, or how one of the Lost Boys had defied him again, or how Tiger Lily played a trick on him.

He promised when he grew up and figured out how, he would come back for her and turn her fin into legs. Then they could marry like adults do and be together forever.

But he never returned after that one summer.

Perhaps if she stared at her reflection long enough, it would bring Peter back and all be real. Wasn't that what Neverland was supposed to be? A place to play pretend, where imagination became reality? But no matter how hard she tried to reach for Peter's imaginary reflection, she always ended up alone, weeping at the lagoon's edge.

Every day, for ten years, she swam up to the surface and sat for an hour, creating stories and fantasies about the life she wished she had with Peter.

But then one day, the face she imagined beside hers turned and kissed her temple with a smile. The boyish grin of a man grown up. He reached out his hand and said, "Come, darling."

And this time, he was real....

CLEANING NEVERLAND

AJ Skelly

Cleaning is such a drag.
Filthy, dirty, I need a dust rag.
Piles of trash over there,
Worse than a dragon's lair.
I think that's dirt on the floor.
Nope. Not just dirt, it's more.
More like mud.
Crud.
Let me get the mop.
Crackle, ouch! Bang, pop!
My foot throbs, quite pained
From the crumpled toy I've maimed.
It's a pirate's spyglass
I should have cleaned in the last pass.
I glare at the offending toy
That belongs to my small boy.
Staring, my frown dips

And a smile graces my lips.
Moving on with my chores
I mop up the muddy floors.
Thinking about pirates and ships,
Of hooks, and swords, and fairy zips.
I bet in Neverland, they have colossal messes.
Dirt and gunk and nobody fesses.
All those little boys
All these little toys.
It's more energy than I can muster.
I sigh and pick up my duster.
Fairy sprinkles are piled high
I swipe at it, and the little motes fly.
"All it takes is faith and trust,
And just a little bit of Pixie—" ACHOO!

IMAGINARY

Annie Kay

T HIS IS THE second day in a row Tommy hasn't summoned me.
The clock on the nightstand reads 1:40.

He's late.

We always play at lunch. We meet under the huge, ancient oak tree at 1:15 when Ms. Lilly brings the kids outside to play. My brow furrows as I realize he's been playing for twenty-five minutes without me, his best friend.

I bounce my leg out of habit. Maybe his class got in trouble, and they had to stay in today.

With a huff, I lay back on Tommy's rumpled mattress so hard my head spins. I stare up at the candle chandelier illuminating the room. The ticking of the clock echoes through my head. The buckle of my suspenders digs into my spine. Something is wrong with Tommy. And I have to figure out what.

Tommy and I have a different kind of friendship. At the age of six, he was the designated "odd" kid at school. No one wanted to play with him. They would run away from him and laugh.

One day, Tommy was so upset, he found a knotty, old oak tree to sit under and hide from the teacher.

Tommy cried so hard his tears puddled on the ground. And then something outrageous happened.

From the puddle of Tommy's tears, I sprang to life. It started with my feet. Water pooled to form them and glided upwards. Next were my legs and torso. The liquid spread to reveal my curly red hair and freckled, pale skin. As it dribbled down, my green eyes formed, and for the first time, I saw Tommy. His dark hair was messy over his olive forehead and hazel eyes.

A smile broke from my lips. "Hi," I said, excited to have a friend. "H-hey?"

I stuck out my now solid hand. "Hi."

Hesitantly, he lifted a hand to meet mine. "Hey?"

I took his hand forcefully, and he flinched. I chuckled. "What's your name?"

"Tommy."

"Well, Tommy, what are we going to do now?"

Tommy jerked his hand away and eyed me wearily. "Where did you come from?" He tried to scoot away, but the oak tree made that difficult.

"Well, you made me, silly. I'm your new best friend!"

"B-but I was just thinking how great it would be to have a best friend."

"Yep." I grinned. "And now I'm here! Only you can see me because I'm yours."

Tommy stared at me for longer than was comfortable. "So you're not real? You're my imaginary friend?"

Something in my chest cracked. I felt a flash of pain. With a calming breath, I had to remind myself that he didn't know any better. This was all new to him. Instead of getting upset, I simply held out my arm. "You can touch me, right?"

Tommy hesitated, then nodded.

I smiled. "Then I am real, and I am your friend."

Tommy sat back and took it all in. I held my breath and hoped he wouldn't make me go away. Instead, he looked at me and smiled. "I always wanted a best friend. What's your name?"

My smile stretched wide. "Whatever you want it to be."

Tommy thought for a moment and then beamed. "Peter!"

"I love it." I grabbed Tommy's hand, pulled him up, and chased him through the playground. We laughed and ran for all of lunch. We only stopped to catch our breath when Tommy's teacher blew her whistle.

Tommy's eyes widened, and he grasped my hand. "Don't go, Peter. Please don't go!"

The crack in my chest started to heal. "I'm not going anywhere, Tommy. Not until you push me away."

Tommy beamed and pulled me in for a hug. "I'll never do that, Peter. Never. You'll always be my best friend."

And just like that, the crack in my heart vanished. I wrapped my arms around him and held him tight. Maybe I needed a friend just as much as he did. I couldn't remember where I was before Tommy. Imagines don't work like that. After we leave a place, we lose those memories. I have no idea how long I've been doing this. But I did know that I did not want to leave Tommy. And from the way he hugged me so tight, I just knew he wasn't going to leave me.

That night while we ate dinner with Tommy's parents, he told them about me. At first, they thought I was great. They acted like they saw me, but Tommy and I knew they couldn't. We played along, though.

We would trick them and play along like they were talking to me. But we knew better. After a few months, Tommy had to stop talking about me to them. They wanted him to "grow up," whatever that means. They thought once Tommy did that, he wouldn't need me anymore.

But Tommy refused to grow up without me.

Every time Tommy wanted me near when I wasn't, all he had to do was think really hard, and I'd appear. We started calling it *summoning*. We had heard it in a conversation between grown-ups once, and it sounded right.

Now, taking my eyes off the chandelier, I stop thinking back to the good old days. I used to have the best times with Tommy. Now he forgets to summon me to play with him. Hopping off the mattress, I begin pacing again.

If Tommy isn't playing with me—and I know he isn't playing by himself—then who is he playing with? Heat flares across my cheeks. He can't be playing with someone else. *I'm* his best friend. Me. And that is not going to change now.

I push up my sleeves and squeeze my eyes shut. If he can summon me, then I can summon myself to him. I picture Tommy in my head, his olive skin that's a few shades darker than mine. I imagine his wild, dark, almost black hair and hazel eyes. I picture them so hard until it's like I can reach out and touch him.

I open my eyes to find a shocked Tommy. His eyes are the size of ping-pong balls, and his mouth hangs open like the first time I saw him. Behind him, the ancient oak tree comes into view. He's in *our* spot. The spot *we* always play in. I ignore his gaping face and move past him to find the culprit. It doesn't take long to find a curly-haired blonde girl. She's smaller than me and Tommy. Her eyes are huge behind her thin framed glasses. She races right through me—an icy cold sweeps across my body. That hasn't happened before. The mystery girl dashes to Tommy. He smiles at her. It makes that cracking feeling in my chest come back.

"Let's play hide and seek! You go hide, and I'll count," he tells her and points away from the tree.

The girl nods. "Okay, but no peeking!" she yells as she runs toward the playground.

When she is out of sight, Tommy turns to me, a lot sharper than I'm expecting. "How did you do that?" Before I can answer, he continues, "Why didn't you tell me you could summon yourself? You're always playing tricks on me, Peter!"

"I'm not playing tricks, Tommy. I didn't know I could do it either."

Tommy puffs and shakes his head. "What are you doing here?"

"I was worried about you. I thought something was wrong." I feel the heat spread across my cheeks at my white lie.

"Liar. You knew I was playing with someone else."

Golly. He knows me so well. But I guess I know him just as well. He was doing precisely that, after all. Nonetheless, I say, "Fine. I did. But you're the one who didn't tell me you had another friend."

At this, Tommy stops. He looks down at his shoes before looking back at me. "Oh, Peter. I didn't want to tell you because I knew it would hurt your feelings."

Tears start to brim my eyes. "Well, you're right. It did."

With a sigh, he says, "I'm sorry, Peter. It's just that... just that—"

"Spit it out!"

"I don't want you around anymore!"

I open my mouth, but no words come out. This time a tear does spill over onto my cheek. My lips wobble a bit before Tommy sighs. "I'm sorry, Peter. I didn't mean for it to come out like that. I just meant that I found a real friend."

There's that word again. "I *am* real, Tommy," I grit out between clenched teeth. My hands ball into fists at my sides.

"I know you are to me, but Wendy can't see you."

Wendy. So that's the girl's name. Even more heat pours onto my cheeks. Frustration ripples inside me, making me shake. "But *you* can see me. That's what matters. That's the whole reason I'm here!"

"Right. You're here because I needed you. But I don't need you anymore."

This isn't happening. This must be some dream. Some terrible, twisted dream. Because my Tommy, my best friend, would not be saying these things to me. Because if he doesn't need me anymore, then—

"You don't want me to be your friend anymore," I whisper. It's not a question. It's a fact. We both know it.

Tommy sniffles and looks down. "Yes," he finalizes. "But it's not that I don't like you, Peter. I do. I just have a friend that I don't have to create. Wendy *wants* to play with me. She thinks I'm fun to be around."

"So do I." I can't bring myself to meet his eyes.

"I know. I wish you weren't imaginary."

Another crack. I'm too sad and shocked and hurt to even correct him. Tommy doesn't think I'm real. He doesn't think I have feelings and a heartbeat. He thinks he can just push me away because he found someone others can see. My chest tightens to the point of pain.

Finally, I look up into his hazel eyes. My friend's eyes. The person who needed me once but doesn't now. I look for the annoyance and irritation that should be simmering in those eyes. Instead, I find sorrow and pain. Something that must mirror my own eyes. And I realize that this hurts Tommy as much as me. He doesn't want to let me go.

"I have to grow up, Peter," he whispers softly. "By myself." It's barely audible over the pounding in my ears.

This is what his parents were talking about . . . growing up.

Well, I hate it.

A strange tingling crosses my feet. I look down to see them start to vanish. It's like water vapor disappearing into the air.

Tommy is doing it. He's letting me go.

"You're turning into water," Tommy says, amazed. "Why is it doing that?"

"I guess I was made from water, so I'm turning back into water." I think about the puddle of Tommy's tears that made me. And now he is unmaking me because he is growing up and doesn't need me anymore. Maybe growing up is a good thing for Tommy. It's just bad for me.

My legs begin to fade away too. A pang of panic washes over me. What if I don't remember Tommy when I'm gone? What if I wake up to a new person and forget Tommy completely? Or worse, what if he forgets me?

With a tight grasp, Tommy clamps onto my arm. "Peter, don't forget me." He echoes my own thoughts.

The panic is written all over his face. This is hard for him, too; I know it is. But Tommy has Wendy now. He will be okay. He has someone to watch out for him. And that is enough. I touch his hand as a silent gesture to release me.

"I won't forget." I hope it isn't a lie. Another tear slides down my face. "I'll remember you forever, Tommy."

I give him a small smile as my torso starts to vanish. He smiles through his tears, relieved to hear my answer. My heart clenches at the thought of never remembering his face. But he believes I will. And that is the greatest trick I can give him.

Tommy drops my hand as it turns to vapor inside his. The last thing I think is how much I hate this *growing up*. I hate it, hate it, hate it. I keep looking at Tommy even when my vision spots and begins to fade. I keep looking even as everything turns to darkness.

I blink my eyes open, blinded by searing sunlight. I place my hand above my face to block out the light and roll over onto warm sand. My head swims with dizziness. The last thing I remember is Tommy's face—

I sit straight up and blink a few times. Tommy. The playground. The oak tree. *Wendy.* I remember! A smile bursts across my face at the overwhelming joy of actually remembering *my* best friend.

A faint jingle fills my ears. I glance down to find the source of the gentle sound. A small light glows on the sand beside my hand. I peer closer to find a small, glowing girl. She has shimmery wings that sprout from her back. Her lips move, and a soft bell-like sound comes out. Strangely, I can understand her musical language.

"Hello," she chimes. "My name is Tinker Bell."

"I'm Peter." I gulp. "Are you a fairy?"

She giggles. "Yes."

"Where am I, Tinker Bell?"

She flies up to meet me at eye level. The fairy spins around and opens her arms wide. "This is Neverland. Home of imaginary friends who hate growing up."

My eyes twinkle. "Neverland?" I look at my surroundings. We are on a beach that stretches into a semi-circle. A bay meets the open ocean for miles across the horizon. In the far distance, I see a ship with black and red sails. "Do other people live on this island?"

Tinker Bell nods her head. "Pirates, mermaids, natives, and fairies fill the land. And you, Peter, are our very first Lost Boy."

"Lost Boy? What's that?"

Tink flies so close to my face that I almost have to cross my eyes to see her. "Well, that's you, silly. A Lost Boy is exactly what you are.

An imaginary friend lost from your person. You are to find others like you and bring them here, to Neverland."

Tommy. My chest tightens a bit from sorrow. But the memories that flood my mind remind me to be grateful. I didn't trick him. I remember Tommy. Forever.

I stand up to dust the sand from my green pants. A hat is lying beside me, the same shade as my trousers. A single red feather is planted on the side. I pick it up and place it snugly on my head. A Lost Boy. The first one. Neverland. A place for imaginary friends just like me who lost their people to growing up.

Staring out into the ocean with the island behind me and my new fairy friend at my side, I take in a heavy breath. "Well, Tink, I think this is the beginning of an awfully big adventure."

The Tale Continues in Volume Two

WHAT NEVERLAND MEANS TO ME

Hannah Carter

When I was younger, I wanted to fly
Right to that second star up in the sky
To the land where I would never grow old
Never have to try and fit into their mold

I could fly with my new friends all day
And things and people could always stay
Swim with mermaids and ride a wave
Play pirates or fairies, pretend to be brave

For you see, I grew to detest change
No matter how we fight it, it's so strange—
It makes friends into strangers and enemies into friends
But how I wish Neverland could help us make amends

No more growing up or growing old; just listen to your heart
No more falling in love or falling apart, a brand new start
Just Tinker Bell, Peter Pan, all of us together
Soaring through the night sky and onward to forever

What's a Lost Girl to do when she can't go home?
What's a Lost Girl to do when she's got Peter Pan Syndrome?
Just a Lost Girl, trapped on the ground
Hoping that one day, she'll be found

Yes, just a Lost Girl, out of faith, and trust, and pixie dust
Just a Lost Girl, in a fight against time that's unjust
Just a Lost Girl, hoping for my chance to soar
Just a Lost Girl who carries Neverland in her heart forevermore.

ICY TEARS

Anne J. Hill

ALONE IN THE dark woods, a little boy sat. Abandoned, left to fend for himself in the great wide world full of monsters and humans who wanted to capture elf boys like him.

He shivered in the falling snow. The trees were the only barrier between him and complete vulnerability. The leaves shielded him from monsters like the father who'd left him and the mother who hadn't cared.

Something crunched in the snow, and he jerked his head up. A fawn tentatively crossed his path and paused to stare at him.

"Hello, little friend." He held his shaking hand out, palm up. "Are you lost too?" He'd give anything to make a friend.

Its nose wriggled as if debating to sniff the pink hand.

He sneezed, and the fawn's ears flattened as she darted away, leaping through the snow.

"Figures," he mumbled to himself and pushed up to stand. Laying in the freezing weather wouldn't help anything.

Pulling his cloak tighter around himself, he stepped in the fawn's footprints and jumped along behind her. She might not play with him, but he could pretend he hadn't scared her off.

An owl hooted from up high. The forest was full of noises. Like the gentle touch of snow landing on leaves or the *drip-drip* of...

Of what?

The snow couldn't be melting already.

He froze when he looked up from the fawn's footprints.

The baby deer hung over a fallen log. Crimson blood dripped from its shredded throat and melted away the pure white snow.

There were monsters in these woods too.

Who could hurt such a helpless creature? What sort of beast could be so cruel?

He shuffled through the snow and stopped by the deer, running his fingers down its still warm muzzle. His eyes filled with tears that slid down his cheeks and froze as if they were already icy.

That was the day he decided no more monsters were allowed in this forest.

His forest.

He spent the cold weeks warding off frostbite until he learned he could make fire with a simple wave of his hand.

Each day, he became stronger in his powers and stronger in his desire to protect the forest.

He eventually grew up and built a tower in the trees. He rid the wood of monsters and darkness and filled it with fruits, sunshine, and happiness. But he was still all alone, just like he had been as a child.

So he invited any elves to come live, dance, and dream freely in his forest tucked away from the world. A place where he would keep them safe. A place where no more monsters could get them.

A wood where the Guardian of the Forest didn't abandon even the fawns.

The Guardian of the Forest will return in Anne J. Hill's novel,
Thorn Tower.

WHAT GROWNUPS FORGET

Charissa Sylvia

No one knows
Neverland
like Peter Pan.
He knows it's true,
that a bird's-eye-view,
flying over sky and sea,
is the best way
to see each shadowed tree,
every strip of sandy beach,
all the shrouded nooks,
and clouded coves,
that beg for a
second, curious look.
He knows up high,
is how you see,

answers to the
most complex mysteries.
Like how the sky,
holds up the stars,
to light the dark,
and shines them brightest,
when things are hard.
He knows by heart,
what grownups forget:
if you can't solve a problem
from down on the ground,
try flying up high,
where the stars are found.

THE LAST HOPE OF NEVERLAND

Hannah Carter

NEVERLAND WAS DYING.

For so long, it had been kept alive by the hopes and dreams of children, but now, as darkness crept into the world, the young ones often tossed aside their whimsical fantasies.

Neverland needed a new host. A youth who would be content, happy even, to forsake their adulthood and come to the land of make-believe. To be the protector of the fairies, swim with the mermaids, fight off the pirates and their grown-up views of the world.

"Hush, my child," Blue whispered to the sleepy infant. She placed her daughter in the flower bassinet as it drifted on the river. This would carry the babe right over the Never-Falls and to London below.

Where the last hope of Neverland might reside.

Such a weighty goal to put on a newborn—to save the world.

But if no host, not one innocent soul could be found...

Perhaps Blue's daughter would find a new home.

Love.

Safety.

Blue placed a kiss against her daughter's soft forehead. Tears dripped into the Never-River as a mother bid one last farewell. "Sleep well, my little Tinker Bell. May you someday come back to Neverland with a savior for us all."

FLY

Rebekah Crilly

Peter took her hand
willed her to fly
think happy thoughts
and take to the sky
become the story
on windowsills told
dance the clouds
and never grow old
"what if I fall though
and hit the floor?"
"but Wendy, Darling
what if you soar?"

STRAIGHT ON 'TIL MORNING

Hannah Carter

PAN WAS DEAD.

Tiger Lily heard it first from the mermaids.

Though they cared little for most filthy humans, they had a soft spot for Pan. Their mourning songs carried across all Neverland that first day.

All of Neverland took up the tune.

Tiger Lily could feel the sadness of the earth beneath her feet whenever she went barefoot through the grass.

Pan is dead, the blades whispered as they bowed their heads and wilted. *Neverland will die.*

Then the cracks appeared.

Tiger Lily found the biggest one by Skull Rock when she went out exploring. Peter and the lost boys often played there.

Instead, she found the gray stone split right in two, like someone had taken a ginormous sword and sliced it clean.

Tiger Lily swallowed as her fingers traced the outside of the deep gorge.

Could Pan really be dead?

She adjusted the bow and arrow on her back. Her dark eyes scanned the horizon. The air seemed still and morose, just as it had been the past week since the mermaids' dirge started. Peter had been a sort of friend ever since he and Wendy first rescued Tiger Lily from Captain Hook, maybe a year ago. Time was so funny in Neverland. Days and nights passed, and therefore, it should be measurable, but Tiger Lily had never aged since Pan had used the fairies to wish her and her tribe into existence so many years ago.

The fairies had created life through their magic, but oftentimes, Tiger Lily wished they hadn't.

It felt like they'd condemned her to a prison from the moment she'd been born. Never to age, never to grow up, never to experience adulthood—what seemed like torture to Pan and his merry band of Lost Boys held such intrigue for Tiger Lily; a taste of the forbidden fruit.

Sometimes, though she'd never speak of it to a soul, she dreamed of plunging Neverland into the seas far below to bring magic back to the bland world London belonged to, just to satisfy her own selfish desires.

But Pan would never allow it, and up until now, Neverland had been his domain.

But if Pan was dead…

Suddenly, there was an opening for the host of Neverland.

Yet Tiger Lily herself could never take up the mantle because she'd been born in Neverland. Her dream remained out of reach, forever sealed off to her.

Tiger Lily ran over the browning grass toward the hanging tree.

"Peter? Peter? Peter Pan?" Tiger Lily peered into the holes, each specially made for a Lost Boy. But she heard no sound of merrymaking down below. "Hello? Is anyone down there?"

The wind rattled the trees.

Pan is dead, the clacking branches seemed to say.

"Who killed him?" she demanded. "Who is responsible for killing the Boy Who Won't Grow Up? Hook? His pirates?" Although it could have been almost anyone—Pan pushed many people to their breaking points—Hook retained the position of archenemy.

Something tugged on Tiger Lily's long, loose black locks.

She spun around and saw a haggard ball of light next to her. "Tink?"

As a magic-birthed child of the fairies, Tiger Lily had no problem understanding Tinker Bell's lyrical language.

"Oh, Tiger Lily. It's true. It's all true."

Tink buried her face in her hands as she settled on Tiger Lily's shoulder.

Though Pan had been temperamental, possessive, and childish sometimes in the worst way—he had been the host of Neverland. He'd saved Tiger Lily's life, despite treating the danger as merely a game for his fancy. She still felt a twinge of despair, of sorrow, though it didn't reduce her to tears as it did Tink.

"How?" Tiger Lily swallowed. She knew the answer before the dark musical note left Tink's throat.

"Hook."

Tiger Lily growled under her breath. "I knew it. But how?"

"Trickery," Tink whispered. "He used Peter's pride against him. Planted a traitorous Lost Boy. Peter never thinks his friends will betray him; he thinks they idolize him. The boy killed him in the middle of the night."

"Let me guess. Hook wants to be the next host of Neverland."

"He made a bargain with the Shadows." Tink sucked in a shuddery breath, and her light dimmed even more.

The Shadows.

The evil reflections of all Neverland inhabitants; the dark, nightmarish side of the beautiful dreams.

For—well, who could measure time, really, but it must have been *years*—Pan had kept them in balance. As awful as he could be, the Shadows were a thousand times worse: the darker side of humanity, those that sought to end childhood by any means necessary. No child would be safe, not in Neverland or anywhere else if the host did not keep them locked up.

"What could Hook gain from them?" Tiger Lily held out her finger so Tink could hug it. The tiny fairy's tears wet the very end of Tiger Lily's nails. "Can he really trust the Shadows?"

"Of course not. But he's desperate to be free of this place. He's been trapped here for so long. Peter stole Hook and his crew years ago, just to be more playthings for Neverland fantasies." Tink sniffed. "Desperation has driven many good men to depravity."

"So Hook takes over as host, releases the Shadows, and . . ."

"Destroys Neverland to be free. I tried to warn Peter when the other fairies told me, but he didn't listen. He thought I was jealous again." Tink clung to Tiger Lily's index finger as a baby might cling to its mother. "And now he's . . ."

Pan is dead.

"We have to find a new host before Hook completes the Neverland Trials." Tiger Lily straightened her shoulders.

Every part of her heart yearned to complete the Trials herself: to steal a mermaid's scale and earn a mermaid's tear; to get a feather from the Neverbird; to be named a warrior true by Tiger Lily's father; and to earn a fairy companion true. But as a born-and-bred resident of Neverland, it could never be. Neverland thrived on the dreams of those from the world below; it would never accept anyone else as a host.

Hook, though older than Pan, qualified to compete solely because he'd been born in Wendy's world.

"He's already captured a fairy companion. Tippy-toe. She vied to be Peter's companion long ago and always hated him for rejecting her—and me for being Peter's favorite." Tink lifted her head. A fairy could only hold one emotion at a time in their small body, and right now, her sorrowful face seemed like her soul might cleave in half. "She's sprinkled the pirate ship in pixie dust, and it guards the second star so no one can fetch a child that might thwart Hook."

Tiger Lily scowled. Fingered her hair.

Stared at the entrance to Pan's lair.

"That sounds like a challenge," she hissed.

Tink flashed. Her light grew brighter as her sadness shifted. She clasped her hands, her eyes alight. "Oh, Tiger Lily! Do you think you can really challenge Hook?"

"I don't see why not." Tiger Lily lifted Tink into the air. "And I know who might help."

Tiger Lily sneaked back into her home among the trees. As her father was the chief, their round, wooden house towered above all the rest in the tribe, save the seven-sided ceremonial building—the Third Star, as they called it. During Neverland's summer, her father cut a hole in the thatch roof to let out smoke; right now, she saw no gray clouds in the sky except from the Third Star.

Voices drifted out, though Tiger Lily could not make out what they said. But she could assume they had discovered what she had:

Pan was dead.

"Dim yourself, just in case," Tiger Lily whispered as they crept through the brush. She knew the path well enough that she made no sound. Not a branch cracked, for that might spell death.

Not just to her schemes but to all Neverland and the world below.

Tink dulled her shine. The girls inched closer to Tiger Lily's dark house.

Tiger Lily's resolve grew with every step. She understood Hook's desire for freedom more than anyone. Perhaps she even sympathized with him—after all, Pan had killed Hook multiple times but always brought back the pirate with fairy wishes, just to slaughter him again.

Because to Pan, the games were far more important than the players. And he could not play hero if he didn't have a nemesis to defeat.

To be caught in an endless, painful cycle of death, rebirth, and death again... Tiger Lily would want to kill Pan for that as well. But the Shadows were darker still than even Pan. And she would not let everyone in Neverland die, no matter how much she hated her prison.

She would not let Hook become the new host, but she would not begrudge him his freedom, either.

Her footfalls and heartbeats mingled like the sound of war drums in her ear. With each step, each beat, her resolve sharpened. Intensified.

She pulled aside the sheet that acted as the door to her elder brother, Atohi's, bedroom. Inside, he displayed many of his weapons on the wall. She reached for the smallest of them—a long knife used for the hunt.

She swung it around to test its weight. It felt different than a bow and arrow, but she knew she could not rely on her trusty weapon to save her should a pirate sneak up on her from behind.

Tiger Lily slid the sheath from the wall and glanced over her shoulder.

Her heart thudded faster, both with anticipation and anxiety, as she reached into Atohi's drawer chest. Her fingers grazed over his leather hunting outfit, the one with the sleeves cut off. Beneath it and his pants sat paint—war paint.

As a female, technically, Tiger Lily should not be allowed to dress like a warrior nor wear the paint as she marched into battle. But this was not a hunting trip or one of Pan's games, and she could stomach no more rules of any sort.

She drew out the blue, her favorite color, and drew three stars on her cheek using Atohi's mirror. One star to represent the world below. The second star to represent Neverland. And the third star to represent her people, the reason she undertook this mission.

On her other cheek, she used the blue, white, and mixed a darker black with the blue to craft a tiger lily flower on her cheek.

For the world. For Neverland. For her people. For *herself.*

"You're a good artist." Tink landed on Tiger Lily's shoulder and peered at the drying paint. "I never knew you could do this."

"And this is what I can accomplish on a short time limit." Tiger Lily smiled, careful not to let her artwork crack too much.

Next, she used the white to draw a line down her cheek and on her lips. This had no particular meaning besides she had seen others do it, and she thought it looked both fierce and mysteriously beautiful at the same time. A fiery inner strength, barely concealed behind a veneer of beauty.

Hook and the Shadows would tremble before her.

With her war paint done, she slipped into her brother's clothes. Even though he had two years on her, she had outpaced him in height since their creation. They stood head and head, almost, a fact that irritated the chief's son to no end.

She twisted around in the clothes and found that they fit her just as well as they fit him.

Now—the final step.

She allowed no weakness as she seized the knife once again with one hand—and her hair with the other.

Her hair, her beautiful hair—a symbol of childhood, of her youth, of her status. But when Tiger Lily looked into the mirror with never-aging eyes—she did not see a fourteen-year-old daughter of the chief. She saw a woman, barely held together by the last threads of adolescence.

She saw a warrior, one who would fix Neverland.

And that warrior sliced through the locks until only a chin-length black bob remained.

Tiger Lily—fierce as a tiger, beautiful as a lily.

Warrior of Neverland. Defender of dreams.

Tink's pixie dust made it easy enough to take to the skies. Tiger Lily perched on a cloud and watched the yellow dust-coated pirate ship soar in the sky and leave a dark splotch on the moon. She could imagine Hook and Tippy-toe, that traitorous fairy, as they whispered in his captain's quarters about how to pass the Neverland Trials.

Tiger Lily wondered if they thought she might fight back. If they even remembered the other person who could easily become the host of Neverland.

Tiger Lily's prey: Wendy Darling.

Tiger Lily pushed off the cloud and flew closer to the second star, with Tink by her side. Their dust-coated skin sparkled like the stars that gleamed above them. Tiger Lily hoped she might use it as a camouflage against the pirates. She prayed they would be so sleep-deprived that they'd consider her nothing but another Neverland oddity, a girl made of stars that floated through the night sky.

Tiger Lily let out a puff of air and sped up. She dove down, below the pirate ship, away from the vantage of any prying lookout. Tink's light seemed almost nonexistent—the fairy had switched to her depressive mood again, perhaps on purpose. Poor Tink flew beside Tiger Lily and wept the whole time, softly, like the solo of the tiniest bell one could imagine.

They passed underneath the hull of the ship, far below. Tiger Lily moved up a little higher, her course set on the second star.

How long would it take her to reach the ground surface of reality?

She could feel the magic intensify, grab hold of her soul and urge her on. She'd never taken this flight before, but she could tell why it felt so intoxicating to Pan. Why he did it so many times, even though he had utter disdain for the world below and its emphasis on grown-ups.

She closed her eyes and felt the short, stubby ends of her hair twist around her face. She lifted her hands up and—

"Captain! Flyer on starboard!" someone shouted.

Tiger Lily hissed and whirled around right before a shot flew by her head.

Tink flashed a bright red. "Go!"

Tiger Lily pushed herself upward, but she could still see a small figure, clothed in black and white, as he tumbled out of the door. Another ball of light hovered at his shoulder, the same size as Tinker

Bell. Hook's fairy companion flashed red, and Tinker Bell's scarlet color deepened, too.

"Take me to the skies," Hook growled.

Tippy-toe swirled around his head; Hook lifted off the ground. He unsheathed his cutlass and narrowed it at Tiger Lily.

"You should have stayed back with your tribe," Hook hissed.

"And you should have stayed back on your boat." Tiger Lily nocked her bow and arrow and aimed it at Hook.

She'd heard the legends of the Wendybird debacle from Wendy herself: how the Lost Boys had accidentally shot her down from the sky.

Perhaps Tiger Lily would start the legend of the Hookbird tonight.

She let her arrow fly true. It soared through the sky as Tink cheered, her body a bright yellow again.

Hook dove to the side; his pirate ship let loose a cannonball. Tiger Lily soared upward, but the projectile nearly brushed the tips of her toes anyway.

She didn't have time for another shot before Hook arrived.

He lunged, sword aimed for her stomach. Tiger Lily unsheathed Atohi's knife—*her* knife—and parried before he could stab her through. Hook might have had brute strength and the longer sword on his side, but Tiger Lily had a resolve.

A mission.

One that didn't involve death, destruction, and Shadows.

She tucked and rolled in mid-air and came around his back. She prepared to jab his shoulder, but he reached over and smacked her blade away and sent her falling a few feet. Tink flashed and swerved down to sprinkle Tiger Lily with more Pixie Dust.

"Thanks, Tink," Tiger Lily whispered.

Another shot exploded from the cannons below.

Hook swung his sword down on her head.

Panic seized Tiger Lily; the attacks were too in sync. By instinct, she thrust her knife up to intercept that; her body seized as she expected to be blasted to smithereens by the ship's cannonball from below. She imagined her shattered ribs, her body torn in two as it floated away in the sky. Bloody rain would pour down on Neverland below, another sign that Pan was dead.

But the death blow didn't come.

Tiger Lily kicked her legs at Hook and sent him spiraling backward in the sky. She turned her head to see why she hadn't died— Tink, that blessed fairy, held the cannonball in her tiny hands. She'd dusted the entire ball to lighten it, and the brave little fairy hurled the projectile back toward the ship. It floated lazily away.

"Thanks again, Tink," Tiger Lily righted herself as Hook stopped tumbling. "You don't have to fight me, Hook."

"I do if we ever want to be free of this blasted place," Hook growled. "I thought that you at least might be on my side, Tiger Lily. You never worshiped at Pan's feet like the others do. Don't you ever feel trapped? Pan never let us fly out of here. We're almost free. The Shadows lent me their power to kill Pan; now I have to repay them. Then we'll all be free."

Tiger Lily brandished her sword to protect herself should he use the opportunity to try and catch her off guard. "You've only caught yourself in a worse trap, Hook, if you think the Shadows will free you. I used to feel trapped by Pan's games. And I want to soar free, away from here, too. But now, I just pity you. You will never be free so long as you throw your lot in with them."

Hook snarled and lunged at her, sword extended. He swung for her neck; Tiger Lily dropped to her knees and swung her foot around. She caught Hook's feet and flipped him onto his back. Another boom, another cannonball—Tiger Lily soared high and out of its reach, back to where the magic of the second star could grasp her.

"I know what you're doing!" Hook bellowed. "That girl can't help you now! I'll have completed the Neverland Trials by the time you get back!"

Tiger Lily steeled her resolve. She could hear Hook gaining on her, but she kicked her feet to propel her faster across the night sky. She knew Pan's directions: she'd travel straight on until morning.

Straight to Wendy Darling's window.

Hook grabbed her foot with his namesake and yanked her down.

The metal pierced through the leather of her moccasin and deep into her skin; she screamed as he jerked her back down.

"I won't let you take away my freedom," Hook growled. "Not like Pan."

"And I won't let you kill everyone for your freedom," Tiger Lily snarled.

She kicked him in the nose with her good foot.

The pirate howled; his metal hook dug deeper into Tiger Lily's foot. She screamed and jerked her foot away. Another cannonball sounded; Tink took care of that one as well.

Hook covered his bloody nose, his eyes on fire. Tiger Lily elbowed him in the neck and cradled her injury. Blood seeped from between her fingers and dropped down to Neverland below, a sickening crimson rain.

For a moment, it seemed like she and Hook might call a stalemate after all. Until Tink flew closer, her voice a high, bell-like peal. "Tiger Lily! Go!"

Hook reached out and snatched the fairy from midair. Tink screamed and writhed from in between his fingers.

"Let her go!" Tiger Lily bellowed. She drifted closer, but another cannonball kept her too far away from her friend.

"Go back to Neverland," Hook snarled. "Don't interfere, and I'll let her go. Nobody has to die tonight." His fingers tightened on the fairy.

Pan's closest, most loyal companion.

Tink had always been willing to sacrifice so much in service to Pan. It should have come as no surprise to Tiger Lily when the fairy's voice came as a soft tinkle next.

"Go, Tiger Lily. Hurry. Get Wendy." Tink's bright eyes met Tiger Lily's. "Please."

Another cannonball sounded, and Tiger Lily dropped. The pain in her foot increased, and she knew she didn't have much longer to think. Hook would only bargain for so long; the pirates down below would hit her eventually.

"I'm sorry," Tiger Lily whispered.

"Save Neverland," Tink replied. She reached out her hand; more pixie dust settled on Tiger Lily's head and hands, as plentiful as the stars. Enough for the trip to London and back.

The gesture felt like goodbye.

Tiger Lily clutched a pile of dust in her hand and cradled it to her chest. She would keep it safe for Wendy.

"Don't do it—" Hook began, but Tink flashed a bright red, and Hook had to turn his face away. Her light grew in brightness until Tiger Lily couldn't look at her friend.

She whirled around and flew toward the second star again. She could feel the heat of Tink's light against her back, like the final embrace from a treasured friend.

Though Tiger Lily flew like a bird with an injured wing, she soared higher. The magic grew deeper in her soul and called her onward and upward, farther and farther from Hook.

The light flickered out of existence.

Tears burned in Tiger Lily's eyes as Tink's loving presence evaporated. Tippy-toe's awful peals of laughter echoed throughout the night sky.

"Tink is dead! Tinker Bell is dead! And we'll kill Wendy Darling and you, too!"

Pan was dead.

Tink was dead.

But Tiger Lily still lived, and she could hear

But somewhere in London, Wendy Darling still lived as well.

Tiger Lily's hope for Neverland would carry her past the second star and straight on 'til morning.

The Tale Continues in Volume Two

SOARING

Anne J. Hill

Soaring with the birds
Above the skyline
Where there is
Nothing to fear

Monsters can't touch you
Up in the night sky
Just close your eyes
Think happy thoughts

Come with me and
Soar through the sky
Past ticking Big Ben
Then on through the stars

Off to Neverland we'll fly
To pirates and fairies
Mermaids and tribes
And time stands still

Me and my band of
Fellow eternal boys
Lost from the world
No nannies or parents

Trapped in a treehouse
With nowhere to run
But don't worry, friend
The fun's just begun...

ACKNOWLEDGMENTS

W HERE DO WE even start? There are so many people that we could thank. Firstly, of course, the authors. Without their stories, without their willingness to not only write the stories but go through extensive rounds of edits... well, you wouldn't be holding a book in your hands.

And, speaking of edits—a big thank you to Brittany Eden, Maseeha Seedat, and Rachel Lawrence, as well as our team of beta readers. You guys are like our editing fairies. You sweep in, sprinkle your pixie dust over everything, and make it just a tiny bit more magical.

Thank you to God for creating our wild imaginations and making everyone unique enough to have their own personal spin on life.

Writing may seem like a solitary job because it's just you, your words, and a blank document staring back at you. But with the amazing team behind *The Never Tales*, it somehow feels a little less lonely. We're our own little tribe of Lost Boys. High-fives all around!

—Hannah Carter and Anne J. Hill

ABOUT THE AUTHORS

HANNAH CARTER

Hannah Carter is just a girl who loves to dream and write and still wakes up every day hoping to figure out she's secretly a mermaid. Hannah's debut YA fantasy novel is due out with SnowRidge press in November 2022. Her short stories and award-winning flash fiction pieces have been published in multiple anthologies, including Havok's *Prismatic*—where she won an Editor's Choice Award. Hannah also won a competition with her short story, "Lara." She currently has two published novellas, *Amir and the Moon* and *Seashells*. In addition to fiction, she also has had over a dozen devotionals published in various magazines, as well as six devotions published in *Finding God in Anime* and *Finding God in Anime Volume Two*. In her spare time, she's probably either cuddling her cats, drinking tea, reading, or practicing for her imaginary Broadway debut.

Instagram @introvertedmermaid3

ANNE J. HILL

Anne J. Hill is an author who enjoys writing fantasy for all ages. Her love of words has also led to her career as an editor and content writer. She runs Twenty Hills Publishing with the help of her circus performing best friend, Lara E. Madden. She spends her days dreaming up fantastical realms, researching ways to get away with murder...for book research, arguing over commas at the kitchen table, talking out loud to the characters in her head while also promising her housemate that she isn't, in fact, crazy, and rearranging her personal library, which has been affectionately dubbed the "Book Dungeon."

Instagram @anne.j.hill.editing
Twitter @AnneJHillAuthor
www.annejhill.com

BEKA GREMIKOVA

Beka Gremikova writes folkloric fantasy from her little nook in the Ottawa Valley, Ontario, Canada, and works as an editor for SnowRidge Press. An avid traveler, she's been to at least six different countries. When she's not trekking across the globe, she plays video games, dabbles in art, or curls up in a cozy corner with a book. Her work can be found in various anthologies, and her twisty short story, "The Other Cinderella," is available now on Amazon and other platforms. Her first book, codenamed Project Dragon, will be released with SnowRidge Press in Fall of 2023. To keep up with all her writing mayhem, you can sign up for her newsletter at bekagremikova.com, follow her on Instagram @beka.gremikova, or join her reader group, "Beka's Books," on Facebook.

Instagram @beka.gremikova
Twitter @DreamofWriting

 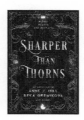

LARA E. MADDEN

She might be crazy—the jury's still out—but Lara E. Madden would consider herself to be widely fascinated, with an affinity for wonder. She is madly in love with Jesus, with storytelling, and with the tribe of colorful characters that is her family and friends. When her feet are on the ground, she lives in Lancaster, PA with her housemate, Anne J. Hill, without whom she would likely never finish any project she starts. She is a novelist at heart but is currently focused on creating short fiction as she hones her writing craft.

Instagram @lara.e.madden
Facebook @Lara Madden
LaraTheWanderer.blogspot.com

EMILY BARNETT

Emily Barnett resides in Colorado with her husband and two sons writing young adult fantasy full of feels. She has had short stories published in online with Spark Flash Fiction and Havok. Her poetry and short works are also in the following anthologies: *Fool's Honor, Sharper Than Thorns, What Darkness Fears, The Heights We'll Fly To, Not the Way You Expect,* and Havok's *Casting Call,* where she won the editor's choice award.

Instagram @embarnettauthor
Facebook @emilybarnettauthor
Twitter @embarnettauthor
www.emilybarnettauthor.com

MASEEHA SEEDAT

Maseeha Seedat is a 17-year-old author, born and raised in sunny South Africa. She made her publishing debut in *What Darkness Fears*, then went on to be the chief editor of the medical podcast Journey through a Stethoscope and the screenplay writer of Maskerade Mystery. Her latest publishing adventure is *Fool's Honor*. When she's not writing, Maseeha can be found chasing after her toddler cousin, hitting the padel courts, or clawing her way toward a degree in physiotherapy.

Instagram @sincerelymaseeha
Twitter @maseeha_writer
sincerelymaseeha.weebly.com

JULIA SKINNER

Julia Skinner is a nineteen-year-old, modern day hobbit, with a love for good stories and chocolate ice cream. She lives in South Texas with her family and two miniature Australian Shepherds (and a ton of other animals!). When she's not working on one of her many fantasy novels or flash fictions, she can be found juggling college, playing video games, dreaming up yet another entrepreneurial project, or happy-ranting about Brandon Sanderson's books. She is a sinner saved by Jesus, and if any good comes from her journey, it's because of Him. Her published works include *Prismatic, Fool's Honor, Casting Call, Darkness & Moonlight*, and more!

Instagram @litaflameblog

TASHA KAZANJIAN

Tasha Kazanjian is currently pursuing her masters in clinical counseling and writes fantasy to escape APA citations. She loves losing herself in books, especially very old ones that smell strongly of ink and dust, and has been known to disappear into used book shops for hours at a time. Tasha's writing process usually involves stacks of historical nonfiction, a hundred index cards stuck up on her wall, and copious amounts of coffee, tea, and colored pens. She is currently revising a dark fantasy novel involving ice age dragons.

Instagram @tnkazanjian.writer

ANNIE KAY

Annie is an aspiring author and accidental poet. She began writing poetry as an outlet, which quickly became a passion. She is a 7th grade English teacher. During her free time, you can catch Annie reading, bullet journaling, embroidering, and playing with her beloved cat, Louis. You can find her on Instagram at:

Instagram @anniekay.reads

CASSANDRA HAMM

Cassandra Hamm is a psychology nerd, art collector, jigsaw puzzler, and hopeless romantic who spends most of her time lost in another realm. As a mental health advocate with a passion for social justice, she writes about shattered girls finding their way in the world. Her two kittens, named after her favorite middle grade heroes, are the lights of her life, and she suspects she may end up as a cat lady (or the owner of a Warrior Clan). Her award-winning work appears in various anthologies, including several of Havok Publishing's collections, *Warriors Against the Storm, When Your Beauty is the Beast, The Depths We'll Go To, Aphotic Love, Exquisite Poison, Fantasea, The Lady in the Tower*, and *Sharper Than Thorns*.

Instagram @cassandrahammwrites
www.cassandrahamm.com

AJ SKELLY

AJ Skelly is an author, blogger, and lover of all things fantasy, medieval, and fairy-tale-romance. And werewolves. An avid reader and a former high school English teacher, she lives with her husband, children, and many imaginary friends who often find their way into her stories. They all drink copious amounts of tea together and stay up reading far later than they should.

Instagram @a.j.skelly
www.ajskelly.com

RACHEL LAWRENCE

Rachel Lawrence writes from South Carolina, where she lives with her husband, four children, and no pets (despite the kids' constant campaign for one). She processes the world spinning around her and the thoughts swirling within her through stories and poetry. Her favorite poets range from King David to Elizabeth Barrett Browning to Taylor Swift. Her favorite Story is still being written.

Instagram @writehereallalong

REBEKAH CRILLY

Rebekah Crilly is not a best-selling author but is working on it. She found her love of poetry during the pandemic and has since been unable to part with it. Through her words, She explores concepts such as parenthood, death, and men's shorts to name a few. You can find her on:

Instagram @rebekahcrilly

BRITTANY EDEN

You can find Brittany drinking tea, reading, and chasing her three kids, usually at the same time. If that fails, you'll find her writing starcrossed romance with timeless endings or on Instagram oversharing pictures of the scenery around her and her husband's home in Vancouver, Canada, and commenting passionately about C.S. Lewis, K-Dramas, Wonder Woman, Bournville chocolate, and Irish tea. Brittany's Heartbooks series of fairytale retellings begins with a winter royal romance in *Wishes* (November 2, 2022) and continues with a vintage tribute to teaparties in *Hearts* (June 6, 2023). Find out more about her stories at Quill & Flame Publishing House or by subscribing to her newsletter From Eden To Eternity.

Instagram @ brittanyedenauthor
www.brittanyeden.com

JADE LA GRANGE

Jade La Grange is a budding writer who has yet to fully discover how exactly she'll bloom in the world of writing.

But while she's waiting, she's on a side quest to live a life that involves vigorously devouring ALL the books, overly-snuggling her precious poodles, spending quality time with her loved ones in the sunshine country of South Africa where she grew up and still currently resides and sharpening the minds of young individuals via her additional job as a teacher with the hope that they too, won't be afraid to pick up a pen and write to their heart's content.

In other words, Jade is still very much a work in progress. And you know what? She's completely content with that. Here's to overcoming life's dragons, one wielded word at a time.

Instagram @madetobejade

SAVANNA ROBERTS

Savanna Roberts is a YA and New Adult author, freelance editor, and the SnowRidge Press co-founder. She enjoys writing stories with complicated characters and hard situations, promising to never provide you with easy stories but ones full of hope. She currently has eight books out and has been featured in the Amazon Bestselling anthology *Beyond the Beast*. In her free time, she enjoys reading, adventuring with her husband and daughter in the beautiful state of Utah, playing D&D, and drinking chai."

Instagram @booksbysr
Instagram @snowridgepress
www.snowridgepress.com

KAYLA E. GREEN

Kayla E. Green is a speculative fiction author and poet in eastern North Carolina where she resides with her husband and furbabies. A daydreamer at heart, Kayla loves creating new stories and building new worlds. When she isn't writing, reading, or taking photos for her bookstagram, she loves singing loudly and off-key to KLove Radio, napping, and pretending she's a unicorn. Her debut poetry collection, Metamorphosis, and her debut YA fantasy novella Aivan: The One Truth, are available through book retailers. Kayla also has work featured in several anthologies. Find her on Instagram @theunicornwriter93!

CHARISSA SYLVIA

Charissa is a wife and mama to both kids and cats living in Pennsylvania. She loves seasons, coffee and browsing old bookstores. She can usually be found scribbling poetry in the bits of time that remain in the day and her favorite sentences start with "then we went outside". You can read more of her work on:

Instagram @charissasylviawriter

OTHER BOOKS BY
TWENTY HILLS PUBLISHING

What Darkness Fears
Fool's Honor
Sharper than Thorns

www.annejhill.com/twenty-hills-publishing
Instagram @twenty_hills

Made in the USA
Middletown, DE
12 August 2022

71236344R00142